THE FIX

A Carolina Connections Novel - Book 1

SYLVIE STEWART

Rolling Hearts Press

COPYRIGHT

ALSO BY SYLVIE STEWART

fix (fiks)

    noun - informal. a position from which it is difficult to escape; a predicament.

    verb - to repair; mend.

    - Dictionary.com

verb - to unbreak shit

    - Sylvie Stewart

Chapter One

PANTS? WHO NEEDS PANTS?

$\mathcal{L}$ **ANEY**

I awoke to a foot in my mouth.

No, not the old feeling of having said something horribly inappropriate that you immediately wish you could un-say, but an actual foot. *In my mouth.*

"Ung guh!" I spat. To say this was a disturbing way to begin one's day would be a gross understatement—emphasis on the *gross*. "What in the … ugh." My head dropped back to the pillow as comprehension dawned. Rocco's size twelve with those cute little toes lay on the pillow next to my face, along with a small puddle of drool. I took in his sleeping form, passed out upside down in nothing but his Ninja Turtle underwear.

"We can't keep doing this, dude," I whispered to myself. My little exhibitionist, having contorted himself into some kind of inverted nocturnal backbend, had spent the night in my bed—yet again. Being awakened by small naked body parts was starting to mess with my head. Not to mention, who knew where those little feet had been? Oh, wait, I did. *Blech*.

Completely unprepared to get up for the day, I snuggled back into my favorite dogwood printed sheets and stared up at the ceiling. I was discovering that moving to a strange new house was rough on a kid. Hell, it was rough on me and I was twenty years older than him. All things considered though, Rocco had been a real trouper since leaving the only house he'd known at my parents' and moving into the cute fixer-upper we now call home. But there were obviously still some kinks to work out—case in point, my rude wake-up call.

When my parents first brought up the possibility of their out-of-state move, I don't think I had ever seen them so edgy. There was lots of hand-wringing and "um, well, you know" before I had demanded they just spit it out—I was halfway convinced one or both of them were dying of Ebola or something equally horrifying.

I'd been feeling increasingly uncomfortable for leaning on them so heavily since the little stick had turned blue, so it was almost a relief to have the decision to get a place of my own taken out of my hands. Turns out while I had feared our moving out would hurt my parents' feelings, they had been afraid I'd fall to pieces without them. One come-to-Jesus conversation later and my mom was accepting a new position at the University of Richmond in Virginia while I was on the phone with a realtor.

The truth is, early on, I would never have survived a day of motherhood without the undying, and most importantly, non-judgmental support of my family and my best friend—as well as the financial, if not physical, support of Rocco's dad. But it was past time for me to pull my big girl panties up and I knew it. All the support I'd received had allowed me to finish my associate's degree and get a job which, while not being entirely stimulating, allowed me to take care of my kid and me. As far as single moms went, my situation was the dream, and I knew it.

Turns out there is something remarkably satisfying about holding ownership of the place where you lay your head at night, and our new house was adorable. It had bright white siding—after a power-washing from my dad—and black shutters that were mostly on straight. And it was topped off by a cheery bright red front door. The house was a ranch and it was a bit older, but it had three bedrooms, two baths, and a fenced-in backyard for Rocco and the dog I was sure we would eventually get. It was close (but not *too* close) to the stores and restaurants, and the street was nice and quiet. I loved it and I was proud of our new home, even if it did have some drawbacks—leaky faucets, a few uneven floors, and *maybe* a few more major problems. But that was okay. All of that could be fixed with time and a little help from my idiot younger brother. I hoped.

On the condition that he would help with the repairs and reno-vating, I had agreed to let him stay with Rocco and me. It was a win-win—my faucets wouldn't drip, and my brother wouldn't be homeless, considering that his previous residence had also been my parents' house. Even he had to admit that, at twenty-two, following your parents to a new state in order to live in their basement was borderline Jay and Silent Bob. And besides, all his drinking buddies were here in Greensboro so there was that …

So now the house was ours and we were making it into a home. What I didn't know before moving was that a new house breathes differently than your old one. It has its own voices and creaky bones to creep you right the hell out if you're not used to them. And we were definitely not used to them—thus the previous month of waking up to Professor Underwear crowding my sleep space in an entertaining array of positions.

It was past time to get out of bed so I laid my hand on Rocco's bare foot and pressed a soft kiss to his head. I inhaled the unique "boy" scent of sweat and the outdoors, trying not to wake him. The floor squeaked under my feet, and out in the hall I tried in vain to avoid the cockeyed floorboard that's entire existence was centered around mocking my lack of coordination. One stubbed toe and several curses later I reached the kitchen and went straight to the vintage avocado-colored fridge for my morning coffee. Okay, what I actually mean is Diet Coke. *Don't look at me like that. There are plenty of people who don't like coffee. And some of them are even over the age of thirteen.*

One could say I am *not* a morning person. As in, I may be borderline vampire. All these people who wake up at the crack of dawn to enjoy a leisurely pot of coffee and read the paper completely baffle me. And don't get me started on those five-a.m. gym weirdos. In my world, no sane person ever wakes up a minute earlier than it takes to frantically throw things together and arrive at the day's destination a mere hair's breadth from being tardy. And usually looking like their five-year-old styled their outfit. And hair.

Armed with my caffeine, I made my way into the laundry room —okay, "room" may be a tad generous, technically it's more of a laundry "closet"—to see if I had somehow managed to wash and dry appropriate clothes to dress Rocco for daycare and me for work in a somewhat presentable fashion. Luckily, the dress code at

Brach Technologies, where I log my 40 hours a week, is pretty laid back. I can usually get away with pants and a blouse or even a nice t-shirt if I throw a sweater over it. Comfort is key if I'm going to sit in a cube all day being hypnotized by my monitor, so my work wardrobe receives almost zero effort from me—much to my best gal pal's horror.

On the complete opposite end of the spectrum, my best friend, Fiona, puts together outfits in a manner I can only describe as "crafting." Copious amounts of thought, skill, and passion are involved when Fiona gets dressed in the morning. Remember the character Cher in *Clueless*? Now you're getting the picture.

Last Tuesday I rendered Fiona completely speechless (a miraculous feat in itself) when she'd picked me up from work and spied the pair of Skechers I was wearing. *What?! They're comfortable! And they were the dressy-ish kind anyway, so suck it!*

The moment my Skecher-shod foot had hit the floorboard of her Prius, Fiona's mouth dropped open, her head tilted back, and she crossed herself, all while doing some kind of deep breathing thing. I had already settled in the passenger seat so there was no escaping the drama. May as well get comfortable, so I pulled my brunette mess of hair into a sloppy ponytail with the hair tie I always keep on one wrist. Let her rant about that one too.

"Dear Saint Jimmy, she knows not what she does. I swear," she muttered to the roof of the car.

"Um, I know who you're talking to and I'm pretty sure he's still alive and well and no doubt creating more toe crushers as we sit here."

"*Of course he's not dead!*" Fiona's head snapped to me.

Oh, it looked like *Exorcist* Fiona was coming out to play.

"I just wanted to apologize in case he's listening," she whispered before clearing her scowl and finally gracing me with her cheery customary Fiona smile. "So, aside from the fact that you clearly got dressed in the dark this morning, how was work?"

Letting her dig slide like I always do, I tapped my index finger to the side of my mouth in feigned thought. "Let's see, ten being a complete lobotomy and one being menstrual cramps, I'd give it a six. Annette brought doughnuts," I explained.

"Mmmm," Fiona mused while pulling carefully out of the parking lot, both of us silent for a moment, contemplating the sheer yumminess that is a perfect doughnut.

"Oh!" she brought her head around suddenly, startling the bejesus out of me. "You'll never guess who I saw on my Starbucks run this morning! For once I know something before you do," she taunted in a sing-song voice before prattling on and gesticulating like a varsity cheerleader with the semester's hottest gossip. "And don't let me forget to tell you about the party we're invited to this weekend—a *wellspring* of man candy, I promise you. God, I need to get laid." Her head tilted back before she straightened again, perhaps remembering she was supposed to be driving. "Anyway, about the coffee thing, I was running late because Gary kept reminding me about needing his half-caff extra, *extra* hot, as if that's actually a thing, so I had to wait forever for the poor barista to get it right and I was just turning around when—" she stopped abruptly. "I forgot. Where am I taking you? Pete's or the other place?"

My seven-year-old Corolla had kindly held onto the last fragments of its bald tires just long enough for me to save for the new ones, thus my chauffeured ride to the body shop. "Pete's. He gave me a better deal on the tires and said he'd try to fix my door dent for free," I replied. *Is there anything more depressing than blowing $300 on tires?*

She looked at me out of the corners of her Gucci-sunglass-covered eyes. "Yeah, and I'm sure it had nothing to do with Thelma and Louise bobbing around under his nose when he gave you the estimate." Her chin raise saluted my "girls." "Did he manage to bring his eyes anywhere above chin level at any point in the negotiation?"

I chose to ignore her little joke at the expense of my rack. If I've told her once I've told her a thousand times, you don't get to have big boobs without having big *other stuff* to go along with it. Mother Nature has some sense of justice, after all. "So, continue with this big news," I redirected her, pulling my drugstore sunglasses from my purse.

Fiona has what I like to call an "Oh look, something shiny!" level of distractibility. Her habit of losing track of thoughts and taking little verbal strolls during conversation can be a tad confusing. Listening to her tell a story is like picking your way through a vocal minefield. But since she's my best friend, I choose to find it charming. As do most people, actually. That's just Fiona—a charming little verbal-diarrhea-spewing pixie with a gorgeous heart-shaped face and wispy blond hair. She is also the most cheerful and positive person I know, and although she occasionally has a temper and definitely has a dirty mind, everyone loves Fiona. Most people would like to carry her around in their pocket like one of those celebrity purse dogs, but infinitely better. However, she's mine and I will never give her back.

"Oh, right," Fiona said. "So, Starbucks ... anyway, the barista hands me Gary's coffee but it's the wrong one and I turn around to tell her mine is the venti black one, not the tiny grande with cream … although why Gary doesn't like a little cream, I don't know."

Something else about Fiona? She has a mouth on her, no doubt, but she also has this uncanny knack for saying things that sound overtly sexual (at least to those of us with dirty minds, so, yeah, pretty much everyone I know), but are in fact completely innocent. And she doesn't seem to know she does it, therefore making it all the more hi-*lar*-ious, especially coming out of that angelic face. It's so bad that my idiot brother and his equally idiotic best friend have a running bet where the first one to get turned on by something Fiona unwittingly says owes the other five dollars on the spot.

"… and I practically run smack into Gavin," I heard her say.

Speak of the devil. Literally. My idiot brother, Gavin.

"Gavin? *My* Gavin? My idiot brother, Gavin? What in the poop was Gavin doing at Starbucks? He doesn't have enough money for a Starbucks coffee. He doesn't have enough money for a complimentary coffee!"

"Well, I know, but give him a break," she chided and then grimaced. "And you've got to stop saying 'poop' so much, Laney. It's kind of nasty."

I waved her off with my hand. "I know, I know, it's disgusting, but I'm trying not to say 'fuck' anymore and Rocco won't stop with all the 'poop, fart, and butt-crack' talk so it's invaded my vocabulary without my permission—like osmosis or something. Forget about that," I shooed. "What about Gavin? You know, he's been acting shady lately, the little bastard, and I know he's up to something that's going to end up costing me either money or pride, and I can't afford either." I rubbed my freckled cheeks, a habit I have whenever I get stressed or nervous.

"No!" Fiona cried excitedly. "That's just it! He was interviewing for a *job*!"

My hands dropped. "Shut your face! At Starbucks?!"

"No, of course not." She waved a dismissive hand. "He'd have to shower for that."

"And wear a shirt," I replied, taking in this revelation.

"And pants," Fiona finished thoughtfully.

Hmm. The source of Rocco's "underwear only" policy was becoming evident.

"So where was he interviewing then?" I asked.

"At some construction company with an office next door to Starbucks. He said something about the company renovating the Harris Teeter on Friendly by my dry cleaners. Not that you would know what a dry cleaner is, my fashion-impaired friend." She gave a little giggle. Why was I friends with her again? "But I digress ... apparently the company is growing really big and they need some new muscle to push it hard on a couple new jobs."

I snickered only momentarily at her inadvertent dirty remark, too distracted by the notion that my beloved ignoramus may actually be growing up and attempting to take on responsibility. *Wow*. I might cry.

This brings me back to my laundry room at 7:15 in the morning where I was sifting through clothes while trying not to spill my Diet Coke. Rocco's wardrobe was a snap: shorts, t-shirt, socks, sneakers. *Bam*. I'm not one of those moms who dress their kid like a tiny grown up in collared shirts and pleated pants with belts and Top-Siders. He's not executing a business deal—he's going to preschool. Where he will most likely get paint in his hair, will most definitely get boogers (hopefully his own) on his shirt, and will quite possibly pee his pants. Shorts and a t-shirt work fine for that.

Aha! I finally uncovered a slightly wrinkled, white eyelet button down for myself that I could pair with my low-rise black pants, kickass silver-studded belt and some comfy ballet flats. Clothes in hand, it was time for me to wake up my little streaker.

Halfway back to the master bedroom, I heard music. Billy Idol, to be precise, his plea to "ride the pony" coming from the extra bedroom where Gavin had been squatting for the last few weeks. The song was abruptly silenced (*thank you*) with what sounded like a cellphone hitting a wall. That was odd. Gavin had the same sleeping-in gene I did so why would– *Yes!* I remembered now— today was Gavin's first day of work! I squeed to myself and executed some super cool dance moves. I may soon be able to afford the $7 bottle of wine. Not that I could tell the difference, but whatever. The morning was already looking brighter.

With Rocco, now fully dressed, settled in at my shabby-chic kitchen table munching on his bowl of Cocoa Krispies—sans milk, of course—there was *still* no sign of Gavin. It had been twenty minutes. Further inspection back in the hall revealed a closed door and a muffled snore.

"Knock, knock." I rapped as I pushed open the door. "I figured I should rattle your cage since eighties rock doesn't seem to be doing the—*Oh God! Put it away!*" I slapped my hand over my eyes so hard I could practically feel the shiner forming, the vision of Gavin's pale white ass cheeks burning a hole through the back of my skull. The only thing keeping the vomit down was the fortunate fact that he was on his stomach instead of his back.

"Guhfmm … what?" came the drowsy male snuffle from the bed, accompanied by a rustling of sheets.

Still shielding my eyes, I whispered-yelled, "Get your hairy ass covered!" I did not want to alert Rocco to any possible distraction involving his favorite person and unfortunate role model.

"Hey, it's not hairy," Gavin protested with a yawn. "You're just jealous cuz mine's perfect and yours is, well, you know."

I turned to face the hall again and lowered my hand. "You can't be late on your first day, Gav. And for God's sake, put on some pants—there's a minor in this house and there is no way to un-see that whole mess you've got goin' on, Billy Idol." Careful not to glance in his direction, I made a vague circular motion with my finger and hurried away to finish getting myself ready for the day.

I returned to the kitchen with five minutes to spare. Gavin, thankfully now clothed in faded jeans and an old concert t-shirt, was leaning against the counter with his own bowl of Cocoa Krispies raised to chin level. He spooned a bite into his mouth and focused on his nephew.

"But why doesn't she like ponies?" Rocco's puzzled expression passed between his uncle and me, his lisp making "ponies" come out as "poneeth." His brown eyes crinkled in confusion while his thick dark hair tilted to the side along with his head. "Ponies are awesome."

Gavin pointed his now empty spoon at Rocco. "I don't think it's that she doesn't *like* ponies, Rock—it's just that it's been too long since she's *ridden* a pony," he said, chuckling to himself at his oh-so-lame joke and giving me a sidelong glance in repressed merriment.

"Ha ha," I responded and then gestured for Rocco to give me his empty bowl and cup from the table. "Your Uncle Gavin needs to quit with the livestock stories and get going to his new job," I told Rocco. "And we need to get a move on, dude, or we're gonna be late for school. Go grab your shoes." I tossed the dirty dishes in the sink for later.

Rocco dashed to the side door to retrieve his sneakers and I turned to face my brother. "Seriously, Gavin, good luck today," I stretched onto my tiptoes to give him an unexpected peck on his scruffy cheek. "Knock 'em dead!"

"Yeah, yeah," he replied self-consciously, running a hand through his unruly mass of dark brown hair—hair that I noted had clearly not been washed on this day. *Baby steps*, I told myself.

We both knew this job was a big deal—a turning point of sorts, I hoped—but not wanting to make him feel more uncomfortable than necessary, I threw a small wave over my shoulder, picked up my lunch bag along with Rocco's backpack, and escorted my kid out the door.

"Yeah, good luck, Uncle Gavin!" Rocco hollered as he hopped down the garage steps toward the car. "Maybe if you do a good job we can go on a pony ride this weekend!" As the door closed behind me, I caught a brief glimpse of the cereal spewing from Gavin's surprised mouth and onto my linoleum floor.

One guess as to who'd be cleaning that up later.

Poop!

Chapter Two

IF IT'S GOOD ENOUGH FOR A CAVEMAN...

NATE

"I think that about covers it," said the nurse, handing over the discharge papers. "Any other questions?" Her pleasant smile passed over my mother, sister, and me, finally coming to rest on my father who was perched on the side of the hospital bed.

"I think we've got it from here." My mother breathed in deeply and released it in a resigned sigh. "Plenty of rest, no alcohol, healthy diet, and no stress—easy enough." She tried for a small smile with limited success, although it was unclear whom she was trying to reassure, us or the nurse. Nothing about this mess was easy.

My father spoke up from his seat on the bed. "Are you sure about this whole *no red meat* thing?" His hand swept up to point a finger at me as if this had all been my idea. "What the hell do you think cavemen ate, bean sprouts? No! I'll tell you what they ate—

meat! And then when they were done with that, you know what they ate for dessert? More meat! And you think they weren't stressed? Of course they were; they were being chased by lions and wooly mammoths and who the hell knows what else as soon as they set foot outside the cave. Talk about stressful." His finger made sure to single out each occupant of the room before his tirade settled.

Bailey stepped forward. "Props to your cavemen brethren and all, Dad, but you're forgetting one *tiny*, important detail," my younger sister interjected, crossing her arms. "They all lived to the ripe old age of twenty and were about four feet tall."

"I'll leave you all to it. Feel better, Mr. Murphy!" The nurse retreated to the hall. I didn't blame her.

It was time to wrap this shit show up. "All right, Dad, let's get the hell out of here and get you home." I put my arm around my mom's shoulder and gave her a squeeze. She leaned into me with a hesitant smile.

"It's about damn time," my dad grumbled.

I couldn't blame him for his less than chipper mood. If I'd had my chest cracked open days earlier and had to endure a week of bland hospital food and plastic sheets, my disposition would be pretty damn sour too. Is there anyone on earth who *doesn't* hate hospitals?

In truth, seeing my old man lying on the bed with his body stuck full of tubes and wires when I'd arrived last week had really done a number on me. His normally robust presence had been completely absent and a frail and extremely, well, *mortal* looking figure had taken my dad's place. The shock of it was extraordinary. After that, it had taken very little time for my brain to catch up with my gut. Priorities automatically began to shift in my mind, and decisions that were once complicated and difficult became simple and quite inevitable. I was home, and I was here to stay.

"Soooo," Bailey began once she and I were seated at the dining table in my parents' home, the same home we'd both grown up in just outside of Greensboro. The topic at hand? The family business. "What the hell do we do now?"

I brought my hands together on the tabletop as I took in the familiar surroundings, my mom's small touches noticeable throughout—the Lladro statues lining the sideboard, the dried flowers arranged among the dishes in the china hutch, and a few of Bailey's paintings hung carefully on the opposite wall. I brought my eyes back to my sister and narrowed them at her. "Not so fast, Bay. I've been here a week—don't think you're dumping this whole thing on me as if I have all the answers. I don't know what the hell I'm doing and you can't play your little 'Oh, I'm such a right brain person so I couldn't possibly do anything so uncreative and logical' game. I'll drag you with me kicking and screaming if I have to."

"Oh, shut up, you pompous turd!" She slapped at my arm. "Have I complained yet? I'm more than prepared to jump in. I just don't know where to start. Dad oversees everything, and I mean *everything*. Nothing is outside the scope of his domain." She sighed and propped her chin up with her hand. "It's just a bit over-whelming."

Bailey and I had spent the last few days running back and forth between our dad's office and the hospital; we were anxious, over-whelmed, and pretty fucking exhausted.

So even though Bailey is usually a pain in the ass, I regretted my earlier tone and started over. "Okay, I'm sorry. I guess I thought you'd have a better idea than I would of the best course of action here. I've been out of the day-to-day picture for a couple years now and you've been working steadily with him so I guess I just assumed." I shrugged.

"Yeah, but I'm the design person. I can put together an interior with my eyes closed, but all the administrative and construction crap is not in my wheelhouse, Nate. I'll help where I can but …" She offered a super fake smile and lifted her hands up in the air. Classic Bailey—trying to be cute.

"Have I reminded you yet today that you were a mistake?" I asked, because I'm her brother and it's my job.

"Nate, I could eat a bowl of alphabet soup and crap out a better insult than that."

I laughed. "Okay, that was a good one."

"I know—I've been storing them up since you've been away. I've missed you, you big asshat." She pushed my shoulder. "And I'll do my best to help wherever I can. Deal?"

"Deal." I pushed her right back and she fell off her chair. "Oops."

I knew she was right and the bulk of the responsibility would have to fall to me. I'd been working in construction in one aspect or another since I was sixteen and could legally enter a job site. Even before that, I had spent many childhood afternoons on the trailer floor of whatever site my dad was working at the time. I built some pretty stellar houses and skyscrapers and, well, superhero hideouts, using Legos or blocks or whatever else I had on hand.

My dad's company, Built by Murphy, was founded by his father and was the family's pride and joy. It was also a legacy my dad made no secret he wished to hand down to his two kids when the time came. Unfortunately, none of us had anticipated that time coming so soon, or so abruptly. Not that any of us were under the illusion that Riordan Murphy would quietly submit to the laid-back life of a retiree just because he had a major heart attack. But he would certainly be taking a step back—or several steps if my mom had anything to say about it. In light of that, someone had to take a step forward, and it looked like I was the only man for the job.

Construction is tough. There's a reason most movie scenes involving construction sites occur during smoke breaks or lunch breaks. It's hard to glamorize dirt and concrete dust, let alone try to carry on a conversation through the deafening buzzes and whirs of heavy equipment and power tools. Hard hats and hard work make you sweat and they exhaust you by the end of the day. But then you wipe your filthy face with your even filthier shirt and stand back to take in your work. And *that's* when the magic happens, at least for me. The bones of a future house, or the foundation of a parking structure, or even a whole damn building stand before you. And you know that *you* built that. *You* helped lay that floor, *you* smoothed that concrete, *you* hung that drywall. Your accomplishment is tangible. And, sure, most days you forget to stand back—you're exhausted and ready to hit the shower or grab a beer, or you have some crappy errand to run. But on the days that you remember, there's no feeling like it.

I wasn't reluctant to adopt the actual construction aspect of the company—never had been—but as I'd seen with my dad, the guy who runs the show doesn't wield a hammer. He spends half his time in meetings and the other half putting out fires. This holds little interest for me and is the main reason I left town a few years back. I didn't want to get sucked into the *business* of doing construction. I wanted to do my job, do it well, and at the end of the day just leave it there and get on with whatever the rest of the evening held for me. Taking his work home with him and strategizing to grow a company is what landed my dad in open heart surgery at the age of sixty. No thanks. But what choice did I have?

It all came down to one thing—family. And worse yet, fucking Irish family.

"Come on in," I beckoned to the kid.

It was the following Monday and I was starting my day at an apartment building we were putting up on the north side of town. I'd spent the weekend at the office and at the company's various worksites with Bailey, still trying to get up to speed. We had a few new crew members starting this week and it looked like the first one had arrived.

So maybe "kid" wasn't exactly the right word for the guy standing at the open doorway. He was probably early twenties, and I had only just turned thirty-one myself. But from the looks of his work history that Bailey had passed on to me, I couldn't think of what else to call him. There was hardly a thing there. What in the hell had this guy been doing since high school?

He stepped toward me in the site trailer, hands in the front pockets of his jeans, a tentative expression clear on his face. He was fairly tall, probably only an inch or two shorter than my 6'2" and I suppose he looked strong enough. Bailey did mention the stellar character references she'd gotten from a couple of the guy's former baseball coaches, I think. At any rate, something made her give him a shot, so I figured I'd just go with it. The kid didn't know shit about construction, that was clear, but that didn't bother me per se. At this point, I just needed all the extra hands I could get, and as long as we kept a close eye on him, he could learn a lot of what he needed to know on the job. Nothing like trial by fire.

"Monroe, right?" I asked him.

"Yeah, that's me. Gavin Monroe."

"Nate Murphy." I stuck out my hand.

He took it and gave it a firm shake. "Nice to meet you. And, uh, thanks for the job. You won't be disappointed."

"Well, I guess that remains to be seen, Gavin." His Adam's apple bobbed but he held my eyes. This could work out fine after all. "Follow me and I'll show you around. You'll have to pardon me—I'm still trying to get up to speed on all these open projects, but I'm assuming my sister told you all about that when she interviewed you?"

"Yeah, she did. I hope your dad's doing better."

"He's hanging in there, thanks." I handed the kid a hard hat as I donned my own by the door of the trailer. "You bring a pair of work gloves with you?"

"No, sir." The uncertain look was back.

"We'll find you a pair." I took a step down the stairs. "I'm assuming those boots are steel toed." It wasn't a question.

"Yes, sir."

"All right, come on, I'll introduce you to Mark. He's the foreman on this job and he'll get you squared away. Not sure if you'll stay on this site or not but we'll play it by ear." I strode toward the closest building, not waiting to see if the kid followed. "And cut the 'sir' crap!" I raised my voice over the buzz of a power saw. "You work hard and do your job and save the manners for your mom."

Chapter Three

THE BUT SANDWICH

*L*ANEY

"Soooo hungry," Gavin whined like the little baby he is. He was stretched out on the sofa with his hands cradling his stomach and his sweaty shirt sullying the upholstery.

"Why didn't you eat any lunch?" I asked from the kitchen where I was helping Rocco with his backpack. We'd just walked in the door a minute earlier and I was equal parts eager and anxious to hear about Gavin's first day.

"I did." Whine. "But they had me running around so much I burned that off by about one o'clock. I forgot how much sweat a human body can produce in a day."

Eww.

"I'm hungry too, Mommy," Rocco said as he pulled off his shoes and left them in the middle of the floor—right by the dried up, half-chewed Cocoa Krispies I'd forgotten about from this morning. Double eww.

"Okay, baby." I grabbed the paper towel roll from the counter and went to the sink to wet a few. "How does frozen pizza sound?" I called to the other room.

"Make it two, and no veggies!" came the response from Gavin.

"Yeah, no veggies!" Rocco echoed.

I smiled. I know I probably shouldn't. But when I didn't stop to think too hard about whether or not Gavin was the best influence on my son, I was so grateful that there was a man in his life on a consistent basis. One who would never flake out on him and suddenly find something better to do. Sometimes it even seemed that the similarity in their maturity levels was, in fact, the very glue that bonded them.

I admit that one of my fears when my mom and dad moved was that Rocco would be left with just me, and I would be depriving him of the opportunity to have loving and reliable men in his life. That was definitely a contributing factor in my decision to allow Gavin to move in with us.

My biggest fear has always been messing my kid up.

I just had to keep reminding myself that, in the battle for Rocco's well-being, a guy who loves him will beat out veggies every time.

As awesome as my kid is, he obviously did not just spontaneously appear in my womb one day—as if my ovaries were having a boring day and said, "Hey, you know what would be fun?" No, he was the result of numerous lime gelatin shots, a hot friend-of-a-friend musician visiting from California, and some extraordinarily bad judgment on everyone's part.

Dominic, Rocco's dad, is actually a nice guy and I have to give him some credit. After the initial, and expected, freak-out when I'd tracked him down by phone with the news every nineteen-year-old guy wants to hear—guess what? It's a boy!—he'd tried to step up the best way he knew how. It had been three months since the fateful deed in the back seat of a borrowed extended-cab truck (*I know—don't remind me*), and only three days since I'd finally stopped Linda Blair-ing my guts out with morning sickness. As I sat on my bed in my childhood room clutching my cellphone, we had discussed possible options—me moving to California, him moving to North Carolina—but in the end, it had just made sense for each of us to stay put. My family was here, and I was midway through my freshman year of college. His family was scattered, but he had just been accepted into a very prestigious music program, and while his family had quite a bit of money, we'd both known that him dropping out and moving across the country for his knocked-up one-night stand would not go over well.

As cringe-worthy as it sounds, we were complete strangers. And while neither of us wanted Dominic to be a stranger to his child, uprooting hadn't been the best plan. So I had stayed here and Dominic had flown out for the birth. And after a paternity test, which his family's lawyer had naturally insisted on, a reasonable arrangement for child support was agreed upon and we worked out visitation. Dominic, even now, didn't make much money, but with his family's resources he made sure we got what we needed financially.

And he does love his son—I know this. But I don't know if he'll ever love anyone more than he loves his music, and that's not what I want for Rocco in a full-time dad.

Now Dominic flies out to take Rocco for a few weeks every year between breaks in his busy touring schedule. And we all forge ahead. But at night when I lie in bed and rehash all the parenting decisions I could have handled differently that day—not to mention all the calories I shouldn't have eaten and all the chores I should have completed—I often wish to the bottom of my soul that our story of mother and son had begun differently. That instead of a duo, we were some incredible kick-ass trio.

I set the oven to preheat and attempted to ease into a group discussion so I could covertly interrogate Gavin about his job. I began with Rocco. "So, Rock, did you and your new friends do anything fun at school today?"

"Nah." He twitched his little nose.

"What do you mean, 'nah'? You were there all day."

Another change since we'd branched out on our own, Rocco was attending a new school—otherwise known as daycare—for the full day instead of the half day of preschool we'd done while living with my parents. Once I'd pushed past the guilt, I could appreciate that this was actually a positive change for him. He'd spent the majority of his time around adults before, and it was high time he made some friends his own age.

I moved to the half wall between the kitchen and the living room to find Rocco mimicking his uncle as he lay in my favorite cushy armchair, hand to his gut and head thrown back.

"I dunno," was his complete response.

"Well, what did you do all day?"

"Don't 'member." He shrugged and twitched his nose again.

Well, how do you respond to that? I guessed it was time to move on to the next topic.

"Okay. How about you, Uncle Gavin? Did you do anything fun with your new friends today?"

Gavin's head came off the couch to fix me with narrowed eyes. "Am I allowed to say I don't remember either?" Taking in my look he said, "Yeah, I thought not. It was okay, I guess. They all treated me like the newbie, as expected. Most of the guys were okay, some of them were dicks—I mean, jerks." He glanced Rocco's way, but the little guy was unfazed. "It was mostly a lot of lifting things and holding this or that while somebody secured it."

"That doesn't sound so bad," I commented. "Where were you?"

"I was at some apartment complex off New Garden, but the boss said they might move me to the grocery store on Friendly or maybe even the commercial building going in at the end of our street. I told him I lived here so I think he might try to put me on that one, which would be cool."

"What commercial building?" I asked, unfamiliar with anything being built by our neighborhood.

"I don't know, some building they're putting up with rental spaces—right at the entrance."

That was odd. "There are houses on either side."

"Don't ask me—it's my first day. Nate said the houses were in foreclosure so they got the properties at a really good price. They're gonna tear them down and put something else up."

Apprehension speared my gut, but I pushed it aside. "So it sounds like you met a lot of people for your first day. That's good," I led.

"I guess."

What was it with guys? Would it kill them to share a little?

"Well, since Mom and Dad aren't here, someone has to say it.

I'm proud of you, Gav," I told him. "I know this isn't your dream job but I'm glad you're moving on."

His sudden frown had me regretting my last statement. *Stupid!*

He inhaled and then sighed. "It's no major league game, but whatever. It is what it is."

"What's a commercial building? Will it sell toys from the TV?" asked Rocco as the oven dinged—time to put in the pizzas.

"Uncle Gavin will explain." I turned back to the kitchen to make dinner for my guys. *Baby steps, Laney, baby steps.*

My phone rang an hour later. Gavin was busy holding a giggling Rocco upside-down in the living room and shaking him to get the pizza to reappear. I was adding dishes to the growing pile in the sink, telling myself I'd get to them later. The number on the caller ID was unfamiliar, but I pressed Accept.

"Hello?"

"Oh hi. Is this Laney Monroe?"

"Yes."

"This is Mellie Jordan from Cornerstone Daycare. How are you?"

Rocco's daycare teacher.

"Oh hi, Mellie! I'm good—how about you?" We exchanged pleasantries.

"I'm just fine, Laney. Listen, I'm sorry to bother you at home. I was hoping to catch you when you picked Rocco up this afternoon, but I think I just missed you. I wanted to touch base on a couple things—nothing's wrong, so don't worry," she reassured me.

"Okay, what's up?" I asked.

"Well, first of all, I wanted to tell you that we all *love* Rocco here. He is just such a sweet little guy."

My chest wanted to swell at this, but my motherly instincts were sensing a "but sandwich" on the horizon—*your kid is great, but he's pantsing all the other kids on the playground and we'll have to expel him, but did I tell you we really think he's great?*

"But," Mellie continued.

Here it comes.

"I'm just the teensiest bit concerned about him, socially speaking," Mellie said.

My hand that wasn't holding the phone went to my cheek and the rubbing began.

"He seems to spend most of his time playing by himself, and when we try to encourage him to join in with some of the other kids he says he doesn't want to," she continued.

Rub.

"I wouldn't mention it since he's new to the school and I know kids can be shy, but we just haven't seen any improvement yet—I catch him looking at what other kids are doing so I think he's interested, but he won't go that next step. Sometimes one of us teachers will play with him to get the ball rolling and he'll talk to us just fine. But not with the other kids."

Rub rub.

"I'm not trying to scare you or anything because this is probably something we'll look back on later and laugh about, but at his age, he really should be engaging in interactive play with other kids instead of parallel play we see with the younger ones. I wanted to ask, does he have friends in the neighborhood or from his old school he interacts with regularly? Am I just bothering you for nothing?" She laughed lightly.

Rub rub rub rub—*oh, Jesus Christ, somebody just bring me a loofah!*

"Um, hmm. Well, you see, Mellie, we just moved to a new neighborhood as well as the new school and we really haven't gotten a chance to meet too many people …" I trailed off.

"Oh, you poor thing—that *is* a lot of change all at once. Rocco probably just needs a few more weeks to get in the swing of things, then. Is he getting a chance to see any of his old friends?"

Crap. How did one explain this? *Of course my five-year-old has friends! There's his uncle who is great fun and is always offering to share his* Playboy *collection. Sure, his brain could probably be traded with an orangutan and nobody would notice, but who doesn't like monkeys, right? And then there are Rocco's grandparents! His grandma lets him help grade exams and tells him all sorts of interesting tidbits about late twentieth-century American history—what kid doesn't love to chat about Vietnam?! Let's not forget Grandpa either—he takes Rocco to the Farm and Fleet to talk to the three-fingered manager about riding mowers, because that guy is the one to ask about machines with sharp blades. And, sure, a couple of these besties just moved four hours away, but there's always Skype and everyone knows that is interactive as hell—nothing parallel in sight!*

Rub.

Yeah, that wasn't going to go over well. Time to fess up.

"The truth is, Mellie, what you're talking about has pretty much always been the case. He's not really been into kids his own age. He's an only child and has always seemed content to hang out with adults. I've tried not to worry about it before. I guess I just hoped it would resolve on its own." *How could I have missed this apparently huge red flag?*

"I understand. And, again, I don't want you to worry. But maybe we could try to help things along a little more. Why don't you ask him if there's a child in the class he would want to have a playdate with? Then you could arrange it at your house so Rocco would be more comfortable and see what happens from there," she suggested.

"That's a really good idea. I will definitely talk to him about it." I switched hands so the other cheek could get in on the action.

"Okay, good."

"And thank you for calling about this, Mellie. It's reassuring to know that you guys are looking out for the kids so carefully." I truly did appreciate it even if this particular phone call added one more turd on the shit sandwich that was my motherhood resumé.

"Of course. You have a great night, Laney, and we'll see you and Rocco tomorrow!" she finished brightly, proving once again that people who work in daycare are born with a different set of genes than the rest of us.

Chapter Four

KEEP CALM AND GO IRISH

NATE

"Lookin' good, old man!" I said to my father as he lounged in his favorite black leather recliner. This was the first time I'd seen him in regular clothes instead of pajamas since the heart attack, and I was relieved to see more color in his cheeks. It had been two weeks since my return to town and almost a week since I'd been back to my folks' house. Work was a shitstorm and I'd been doing my best not to bother my dad any more than necessary, but it was nearly impossible to decipher whatever organizational puzzle he worked by. Bailey and I were having a hell of a time keeping our heads above water. Not that we would ever tell *him* that.

Remote in hand, he paused the football game he was watching and turned to me with a hopeful expression. "For the love of God, please tell me you brought something to eat that doesn't taste like cardboard." It was no secret that my mom's cooking wasn't stellar on a good day, so I could only imagine what it tasted like with all the salt removed.

"Sorry." I held my hands up to show they were empty. "Mom only let me visit on the condition I brought nothing into the house that you might find even remotely edible. I got a TSA pat-down from her in the foyer."

"Eh, I figured as much." He settled back into the chair. "Distract me, then. Tell me what's going on at work. Did Mark get that permit squared away? I've got the number of that guy at the—"

"All taken care of," I interrupted.

"Yeah, but we'll be in deep shit if every 'i' isn't dotted on that one," he insisted.

"I know. Mark and Doug have both been a big help, and Bailey knows a lot more than she led us to believe, so we're handling it. I promise we'll keep you in the loop and let you know if we need help. I've already called you a dozen times with questions, and I may be permanently banned from the house if Mom catches us talking shop," I warned. "That was another condition for my visit. She should consider a stint with the Secret Service if this whole retirement thing doesn't work out. Was she such a ball-buster with her students? If so, I'm starting to worry about what may have actually been in all those homemade cookies they used to send home with her." That got a smile out of him.

"Your mother's a saint." He un-paused the game.

"Yeah, I know. What's the score? Are we winning?"

He gave me a disgusted look. "Of course we're winning. We're the Irish."

At halftime I went in search of my mom and some doctor-approved refreshments. She sat at the kitchen table swiping at her iPad.

"Hey, Mom."

She held up her hand as if to stop me while her eyes stayed on the tablet. "Nathan, don't even think about asking for a beer. Your dad cannot have alcohol no matter what kind of pathetic faces he tries to make."

I grinned and went over to kiss the top of her head. "I wouldn't dream of it," I reassured. "What are you reading?"

"Oh, just looking for some healthy recipe ideas. Nothing I've made so far has been a hit and I never realized how much sodium is in pre-packaged food. It's ridiculous!"

She shifted her attention my way and caught my eyes. "Sorry —enough of that. I want to hear about you. How are you, Nate? Are you and Bailey hanging in there?"

"By our fingernails, but yeah, we're doing fine. Don't worry."

"Anything I can do to help?" She tilted her blond head.

"Sure. You can get one of those stupid 'Hang in there' cat posters and give it to Bailey—it'll be hilarious to watch her try to be polite when she opens it." I smiled.

She slapped the back of my hand and scoffed, "Don't torture your sister."

"I'll consider it. I suppose it *would* free up some time in my schedule."

Her hand went to my arm more gently this time. "I know your dad can't say it yet, but you need to know that we both appreciate so much that you came home to take over." Okay, I guess it was time for the serious portion of the visit. "It's no secret that this wasn't your plan, at least not yet, so I wanted to say thank you again. I don't know what we would do without you." She started to tear up.

"Whoa, whoa—no need to get all mushy. You know I'm happy to do it. And besides, I'm not *really* taking over. Dad will be back when he's feeling better." She scowled at me so I hurried on, "I mean, I know it won't be full-time like before, but still."

My mother shifted in her chair. "I know. There is no way he'll give up the business completely, but you know your dad doesn't do things by half measure. I'm just afraid he'll gradually ramp things up until we're right back where we started, and we may not be so lucky next time." She had a point. "So that's why we need to use this recovery time to find him some hobbies."

Say what?

"The doctor said there are plenty of activities he can do that are great for keeping blood pressure down and can be quite engaging. I'm hoping if he becomes interested in something else he might not be so eager to dive back into the deep end."

"Like what?" I asked, picturing my dad playing croquet or painting tiny military figurines with a little brush and a monocle. Inside my head I chuckled—outside I was the picture of serious reflection.

"Oh, you know, putting together jigsaw puzzles or collecting coins or stamps. Or painting landscapes. There are all sorts of things." Her excitement was palpable.

Oh wow. This was going to be fun.

"I've got one," Bailey howled. "We can get him some gardening clogs and a subscription to *Home and Garden.*" Bailey and I were swapping new hobby ideas for Dad between fits of hilarity, picturing the ultra-masculine force of nature we knew as our father in an array of awkward scenarios. All of them included our mom cheering on the sidelines. So far the best one involved the Westminster Kennel Club and some dog trimming shears.

"You *cannot* tell Mom about this conversation," I reiterated, sitting across from her desk and trying to school my features.

"Duh, you shit head," came her clever response.

It was Monday morning and we were supposed to be going over some bid paperwork for an upcoming meeting with a potential client, but I could not resist sharing our mom's plan from the weekend.

"Oh," Bailey started, finally getting us back to business, "I forgot to tell you. Doug called with some potentially troublesome news about the foreclosure properties on Old Oak Ridge. It seems the neighbors are not taking too kindly to having a commercial property in their midst. In his words, 'Trouble is a-brewin'.'"

I waved her off. "Tell them to take it up with the zoning office. Everything is in order on our end. If they don't like it, tough. Tell them to move."

"No, dear brother of mine, *you* get to tell them all of that. Why do you think I'm telling you? You're going to be there anyway when the crew starts the tear down on Thursday so there's no need for little old me to butt in." She smiled sweetly.

"Thanks." I smiled back, a tad less sweetly.

Meetings concluded for the day and all phone calls and e-mails returned, I finally walked in the door of my apartment just after eight o'clock. I had done a grocery run the night before so at least I knew there would be something to eat in the fridge. And beer, thank Christ. As anticipated, I had yet to get my hands dirty since I'd been back in town and it was making me irritable. I just needed a night to sit on the couch, watch some TV, and drink a beer.

Thankfully, I now *had* a couch, which hadn't been the case last week. I had chosen to rent a place until I found time to shop for a house or condo and settle in more permanently. My mother, of course, had offered my old room. Yeah, not gonna happen. And I would have considered staying temporarily with Bailey but then I remembered that she was *Bailey* and I concluded that my own place would be just fine.

Most of my furnishings and belongings were in storage back in Austin where I lived for the last two years. When I'd gotten the tearful call from my mom about my dad, I dropped everything and got on a plane. Luckily, a job I'd been working was just wrapping up, so I wasn't leaving a bunch of loose ends. But there was still two years' worth of my life I just left hanging.

Some of my buddies back there kindly offered to move my stuff into storage for me and I had to break my lease, but the landlord liked me and was a big-time family man himself, so he hadn't penalized me like he could have. It didn't hurt that I'd helped him put a deck on his house last summer and his wife was always giving me cookies and stuff. We had a good relationship. In fact, I had several good relationships and a pretty sweet life in Austin. I was sad to leave.

After watching the game with my dad this past weekend, I had moved a couch and a few other old furnishings from their basement to my apartment. I figured it was enough to tide me over until I found a new place and could get my things from Austin moved permanently. Hopefully, once things calmed down a bit, I'd have time to search for a better place. This one was kind of a shithole, but it was cheap. And for the moment I was content with borrowed furniture, beer, and TV.

Halfway into my IPA and an episode of *Ice Road Truckers* my cellphone rang. I glanced at the screen.

Shit. Reagan.

I muted the TV and answered the call, "Hey Reagan, what's up?"

"Nate! Oh my God, it's so good to hear your voice!"

"Yeah, you too. What are you up to? How are things back in Hippie Haven?"

Her voice lost its initial excitement. "They suck without you, Nate. I miss you."

And that right there was what I'd been afraid of. It was the reason I'd avoided her calls for the past week, although I kept promising myself I'd call back when things lightened up. Reagan was a really nice girl. Honestly. And she made it clear she found me to be a nice guy too. But I suspected she also thought I was *the* guy. Reagan was sweet and pretty hot, she was definitely not *the* girl. Who even knew if any such girl was out there, but I knew for sure that Reagan was not it.

We met at a bar a few months before I'd moved away, and we'd been casually seeing each other since—*casual* being the key word. I was very upfront with her because the last thing any guy wants is girl drama. But then I started noticing some big fucking red flags. She left some of her things at my apartment, and when I mentioned them she tried to laugh it off. Then I heard one of her friends ask about her boyfriend and at first I thought, *oh shit, is some guy gonna jump me for banging his girl?* Until I realized they had been talking about me. I tried to back off and I even sat her down for a conversation about it, but nothing stuck. I'd been planning to break things off completely when my dad's heart attack hit and all hell broke loose.

"Aw, that's sweet." I didn't know how the hell else to respond. "Oh hey, I've been meaning to thank you for sending those boxes. You really didn't need to trouble yourself." She had evidently shown up at my place while my buddies were packing up my shit. She implied to them that I'd asked her to send some of my clothes and personal items, which I most definitely hadn't. She packed up a few boxes and sent them my way. It was nice to have some of my own stuff, no doubt, but the way in which I'd received it signaled nothing but trouble.

"Of course! I knew you'd want some of your stuff and I wanted to do something to feel like I was helping out. How is your dad?"

See? Really nice girl.

"He's doing a lot better, thanks."

"Oh good. So, listen, I was calling cuz I really wanted to hear your voice, but also because I was thinking of coming out to see you …"

Christ on a bike, there it was.

"Oh, Reagan, wow." *Why didn't I break things off before I left?* "Uh, that's really nice of you to think of me. The thing is … work is really crazy right now." *Just tell her the truth, asshole!* "I mean, I'm working all sorts of late hours and between that and checking on my folks ... I don't think now is the best time," I finished lamely like the big fucking coward I am.

"Oh. Sure, I mean, I understand. It's just, you know, I was thinking I could maybe combine it with a trip to the beach too— you know, soak up some rays before the summer is completely over and all that," she tried again.

I started to sweat.

"I just don't think it's a great idea right now." *Or ever. Just say it—or ever.*

Silence.

"Okay, no big deal. It was just a thought!" she finally replied, her discomfort evident. "Well, you let me know if I can send anything else or if you need something."

"I will. Thanks for calling, Reagan. And for all your help. Really."

"No problem." Her voice was quiet. "Bye, Nate." She hung up.

God, I'm such a douchebag.

Chapter Five

WANTED: ONE PLAYDATE – WILLING TO BEG

*L*ANEY

Suffice it to say, my talk with Rocco regarding a potential playdate did not go well. In fact, it didn't even go at all. I waited a couple days after Mellie's phone call to broach the subject, and like a moron I'd chosen to do it as I was getting him ready for bed one night.

"What are you looking forward to doing at school tomorrow?" I opened with, helping him pull his pajama shirt over his head. Why we even bothered to put PJs on every night when they just ended up on the floor twenty minutes later, I don't know.

"I don't wanna go to school tomorrow." He frowned and twitched his nose.

"You don't? Why not?"

"I don't like school." His eyes started filling with tears and there was that nose twitch again. *What in the hell was that all about?*

"But school is fun," I tried. "You get to see your friends and play with toys and run around on the playground. You love all that stuff."

"I wanna stay home with you." He sniffled and I dabbed at his eyes with a tissue from the box by his bed.

"But, buddy, I won't be here. I have to go to work." *Kill me now.*

"Then I wanna stay with Uncle Gavin."

"Baby, Uncle Gavin has his new job, remember?"

"I miss Grandma and Grandpa!" Out came the full-fledged wail. "And I hate school! I'm not going anymore!"

Whose brilliant idea was it to do this at bedtime? It's like I was a damn rookie or something.

Since that had been an epic fail, I decided yesterday to send a quick e-mail to Mellie asking if she could suggest a good candidate for a playdate. I was surprised when I received a response almost immediately (again with these daycare teacher genes—the e-mail even had a winky smiley face emoji and an inspirational quote at the end of it).

Tucker Peterson, she'd suggested. I had my mark.

My alarm went off ten minutes earlier than usual in the morning and I managed to get Rocco to school several minutes early, thank you very much. A Tootsie Roll had provided sufficient motivation to get him in the car that much faster than usual. As every parent knows, bribery is an essential tool useful in preventing the explosion of one's head.

I stood by the classroom door, determined to find my target. I had a vague recollection in my mind of Tucker's mom from the first day I'd brought Rocco to school. If memory served, she had blond hair and was fairly tall and thin. *Aha*, there she was! And there was Tucker at her side.

Good God. Of all the rotten luck.

The child wore a polo shirt with the collar popped and, I kid you not, seersucker pants. Oh, I'm sorry, *slacks*.

What five-year-old even owns— Okay, don't judge, Laney. They are probably great people. Super, even. I gave myself an inner smack to the head and approached with a smile.

"Hi, are you Tucker's mom?" I did my best to gush.

She turned to me and smiled in return. "Yes, I am." *See? This was going well already.* "I'm sorry, I don't think we've met."

"I know. I'm Laney Monroe. My son, Rocco, just started here a few weeks ago." I gestured to my son who was—wait, what *was* he doing? He appeared to be cramming his entire body into his cubby. *Shit.* I quickly looked back to her, hoping she hadn't noticed my kid being, well, weird. No such luck.

"I'm Bess Peterson," she responded, a little less brightly than before, but she did extend her hand which I enthusiastically shook. Ugh. She did the limp-fish-partial-shake which made my very firm —and very normal—shake come off as trying way too hard. My left hand began its ascent to my cheek for a good rub but I stopped it, thank God, before things got even more awkward.

"It's so nice to meet you, Bess. Listen, I know you probably have to run, but I wanted to invite Tucker over for a playdate this weekend with Rocco." I glanced down at her son with a smile that was probably coming off as a little crazy at this point. But he wasn't paying attention to me. He was busy with a finger up his nose while the other hand played with his crotch. *See? Our kids have so much in common already!*

"Oh, that's really sweet of you to ask, but I think we're all booked up this weekend," she said, with what really did sound like genuine regret. All right, let's not give up yet.

"Oh, I understand. Things can get a bit crazy trying to cram everything in after the work week." I made some odd zinging sound—or maybe it was more of a whistle—either way, I was sounding like an absolute moron. I couldn't have stopped my hands from coming to my cheeks if you'd paid me a gazillion dollars. Still, obviously not satisfied with my current level of humiliation, I continued, "How about next weekend?"

"Gee, I—" She stopped and shooed Tucker toward his cubby— on the opposite end of the wall from Rocco's, mind you. "Have a good day, sweetie!" she called after him and then turned her smile back to me. "We usually seem to have lots of things scheduled on the weekends, but I'll check our calendar and get back to you. Sorry, I really do have to run. It was nice meeting you." And she was gone.

Note to self: arrange playdates via e-mail in the future.

Taking my own advice, I stopped in Mellie's office on the way out the door to get a list of e-mail addresses for a few more moms. Armed with new candidates, I drove to work mentally drafting my incredibly charming e-mails I would send over my lunch hour to secure a friend for Rocco.

By the following Monday it was evident that the moms at daycare were all big fat bitches. Okay, maybe that was a bit harsh. It's hard to accurately judge tone over e-mail, and I certainly hadn't emailed *every* daycare mom, but still. What were all these kids doing on the weekends that they couldn't squeeze in an hour or two to play? Was there some big Mensa convention I didn't know about? More likely, there was a giant sale at the mall on child-sized penny loafers and actual polo ponies. *Okay, that was a bit judgy.*

By the time I got the fifth rejection e-mail the picture was becoming clearer. All these kids had been in school together since they were in diapers. They had their little established playgroup and apparently the membership roster was all filled up. It was like *Heathers* for the nose-picker set.

I supposed I could try to reach out to some of the parents from Rocco's old school but that just seemed even more awkward. If he hadn't played with their kids when he had seen them every day, why would they want their kids to come over to play now?

Grrr!

My internal rant was interrupted by the sudden appearance of Annette's curly head over my cubicle wall. "I have the perfect guy for you," she announced. "I'm setting you up and I will not take no for an answer."

"Um, hello to you too."

Annette continued without acknowledging me, "His name is Alex and he's twenty-nine. He has a seven-year-old daughter—divorced—him, not his daughter. He just started at Dan's work and he is *really* cute. I made Dan grill him about his personal life and he is, quote, 'feeling like I'm ready to start dating again.' It's perfect, but I promised Dan I'd get your permission before giving him your number. Say yes." She pushed her glasses up on her nose and put on an overly bright smile while nodding her head and trying to get me to follow suit.

I guess I could use a distraction. What the hell.

"Fine."

Week two of Gavin's job and he was still employed—woohoo! We had just finished an early dinner and I was determined to get Rocco in the bathtub tonight if it killed me. It had been a couple days—all right, five days, *don't judge me*—since he'd bathed and he was getting ripe. In between showing Rocco mouthfuls of mashed potatoes at the dinner table, Gavin had shared a few details of his day.

In my mind it played out like a little show I called *Gavin Goes to Work*, such was my excitement about his new job. There was even a jaunty theme song—*I understand, I need a hobby.* My brother may be an idiot, but he was *my* idiot, and when it came down to it I just wanted him to be happy. It sounded like the job was going pretty well and his overall good mood boded *really* well.

I was just about to start the bath water when the doorbell chimed a painful warbling sound. One more item to add to the growing fixer-upper list.

"Gav!" I yelled to my brother. "Can you start Rocco's bath for me?" I headed for the front door.

On the front porch was a tow-headed boy who looked to be around Rocco's age, standing next to a smiling woman with auburn hair pulled back in a ponytail. The woman was tall, probably three inches taller than my 5'5", and she was dressed in black yoga pants and a dry-fit workout shirt in a bright fuchsia. The boy was holding a toy gun in one hand and a—hmm, was that a machete?—in the other. He smiled up at me with a gummy grin, his two front teeth missing.

"Hi there!" the woman greeted with a very thick Southern accent—not North Carolina thick, Texas thick. "I'm Charlotte Baker, your neighbor from just down the street." She pointed to her left. "This is my son, Aiden. We just wanted to introduce ourselves and welcome y'all to the neighborhood!"

"Do you like guns?" Aiden asked me.

"Hush," Charlotte said. "Sorry, his grandpa collects antique guns."

Understanding the world of young boys, I glossed right over it and put out my hand. "Hey, I'm Laney Monroe. It's nice to meet you. I have a five-year-old son so I'm familiar."

"Oh, that's great!" Charlotte shook my hand—no limp fish evident. "Did you hear that, Aiden?" Then back to me, "I'll bet they'd get along real well then. Aiden's six."

Ding ding ding! Was that the sound of a playdate calling?

"I'm sure they would," I returned, before briefly considering calling Rocco out for an introduction. The likelihood that he'd emerge from the hall naked stopped me, though, as it would prove a tad more awkward than NRA talk. "We'll have to arrange something." I made sure to keep my smile just this side of crazy. Sorry, lady, you're not getting off my porch without a commitment.

"Did you know that a samurai sword can cut a man's hand off in one swing?" asked Aiden.

Charlotte's plummeting comfort level was palpable. "What has your daddy been lettin' you watch on YouTube?"

Eyes on the prize, I let it slide like water off a duck's back.

"Whatever it is, I'm sure my brother has let Rocco watch worse. Boys will be boys and all that." Good grief I was laying it on thick.

"Oh, don't they just beat all?" she drawled. "I think I like you." She beamed at me, and God almighty did I beam right back. I think I liked her too.

We chatted a bit longer until she brought up the second reason for her visit.

"I wanted to ask if you've heard anything about this buildin' that's supposed to be goin' up by the entrance to the street." She pointed again in the direction of her house.

"Um, I think I may have heard something about that," I hedged, praying that Gavin was safely ensconced in the bathroom with Rocco and would not overhear.

"Some of the other parents and I have been lookin' into it a little and we're a bit concerned. Who knows what kinds of businesses are buildin' there. We don't want some bar openin' up so close to us, or anything really that'll mean a bunch of strangers hangin' around or loud noise at night. Not to mention the extra traffic on the street while our kids are out playin'."

I had to admit, some of the same thoughts had occurred to me since Gavin first brought it up last week. I'd just bought this house, and although I got a good deal because of the work it needed, I didn't want to watch its value go down. And of course I wanted to live in a safe neighborhood, especially with Rocco to consider.

"It's been difficult to get much information over the phone, so those of us who can make it were plannin' on goin' over there early Thursday mornin' to try and get some answers. That's when they're gonna start tearin' down the houses."

"Mmhm," I made a noncommittal noise.

"Anyway," She put her hand briefly on my arm. "It would be great if you could make it. I'm plannin' on headin' over around seven to try and catch them early, and I know a couple other people who are comin'." Her face brightened again. "Oh, hey, and we're also gonna have a little get-together this Saturday at our house with some of the other neighbors and their kids. You should come along and bring Rocco! The kids will probably just play on the X-box or run around the yard while we talk about some of the neighborhood stuff but it should be fun!"

Victory! My weekend playdate!

"That sounds great!" We exchanged phone numbers before she and Aiden went off with a wave.

"Soooo," I said, entering the bathroom where a very naked Rocco was splashing in the tub. "Guess who just scored you a playdate with some cool neighborhood kids and an X-box?" I crowed. "Me! That's who." I may have tried out a couple of my cool dance moves too. *Why hadn't I ever taken a hip-hop class?*

"Just, no," Gavin said from his perch on the closed toilet seat.

I loved most everything about my little house, but I had to admit the hall bathroom was a bit small. It had a tub/shower combo, a toilet, and a tiny pedestal sink. Unfortunately, both the toilet and the sink were pink. I'm a girl and even I was slightly offended.

"What's an X-box?" Rocco's dark head tilted back and his face got scrunchy.

"Trust me, kid. You want to play X-box," said Gavin. "It's an electronic game you can play with other kids. It's awesome—and you can usually kill stuff." Hopefully they wouldn't be playing *those* games—although since it was Aiden's game ... yeah.

"What kids?" Rocco still didn't look sold on the idea. And there was the nose twitch again.

"Some of the other kids who live in our neighborhood. I just met one of them—his name is Aiden and he's six," I enthused.

Rocco's head tipped back down and he dive-bombed his privates with a plastic shark. I gave Gavin a side glance.

"Sounds fun, Rock. You should totally go," he offered before standing up. "Well, I'm out." And he left the overcrowded bathroom.

"Will I hafta talk to them?" Rocco asked, zooming the shark through the bath water.

"I guess. I mean, at least a little. Why wouldn't you want to?"

"Do I hafta play with them and stuff?" Another damn nose twitch.

"That's kind of the whole point, baby." *Someone please give me the code to my kid's brain.*

"Oh." Still with the shark. "Nah, I don't wanna go."

"I'm gonna be there too," I kept with the sales pitch. "The other grown-ups and I will be talking and doing adult stuff but I'll be right there the whole time."

"In the same room?" I got his eyes again, along with another twitch. *What are you so worried about, little man?*

"Probably in the next room but you can come see me whenever you want."

"Hmm." His tiny lips shifted to the side in thought. "I guess."

That was the best I was gonna get so it was time to move on. "All right, dude, let's get this hair washed and then I'll let you stay in for ten more minutes—but then you *have* to get out, no arguments." With the amount of time this kid liked to spend in the bathtub you'd think he was a beleaguered mother from a Calgon commercial.

Out in the hall, I stopped at Gavin's open door. He was standing barefooted by the dresser fiddling with his phone, still dressed in his dirty jeans and t-shirt from work, his shaggy brown hair matted from his hardhat.

"I don't get it. What kid doesn't want to go on a playdate? Didn't you always want to hang out and do boy stuff when you were his age? I was always hanging out with other kids, wasn't I?" I asked him. Maybe I was having some selective memory problems.

Without looking up from his phone he responded, "Sure, I guess." Ever the skilled conversationalist.

Rocco's voice floated from the bathroom, singing a made-up song about armpits. "Be honest, Gav. Is Rocco, I don't know, a bit *odd*?"

His head still tilted down to his phone, only his eyes lifted to mine. "Are we both hearing the same noises coming from the bathroom right now?"

Chapter Six

DEAR SUPERMAN: YOUR BROTHER'S A DICK

LANEY

Thursday dawned bright, and I mean *bright*. A person was not meant to get up this early. I stumbled around my bedroom, having woken up without my little sleep buddy beside me for the first time since we'd moved. *Oh, sweet progress!* My alarm had gone off early because I wanted to get Rocco and myself ready for the day and still make it to meet Charlotte at the building site before rushing to school and work. This was going to be a three Diet Coke morning for sure and I needed my caffeine fix stat.

Last night, I had spent some time on the internet looking up nervous tics to see if Rocco's new nose twitching thing was something to worry about. Turns out yes and no. It seems these little tics are really common in young children, boys especially, and they tend to go away over time. Unfortunately, my research also revealed that the impetus for these kinds of tics was often a feeling of general stress. So, in a way, it told me what I already knew. *Ugh.*

After a quick shower and a rush-through of my usual hair and makeup routine, I tucked my hair behind my ears and called it good. Congratulating myself for setting out clothes the night before, I slipped on a pair of charcoal dress pants with a skinny red pinstripe and a V-neck sleeveless blouse the color of a poppy. I paired this with some very low heeled open-toed shoes in a matching color. Even Fiona would approve.

I went to wake Rocco but found his bed empty, firetruck sheets in a rumpled mess and pillow missing. After a search of the living room and kitchen I checked the only other possible place. Yep. There he was, snuggled up next to my brother, firetruck pillow cradling his head and all of Gavin's covers bundled around him. My brother lay next to him, curled in the fetal position with no covers but, thankfully, some boxer briefs to protect my eyes from the bleach bath they would have needed had things gone differently.

"Your son stole my covers," grumbled Gavin in a sleepy murmur.

I smiled—only because my kid is cute, not because I enjoy my brother's pain—and went over to the bed to get Rocco.

"Hey buddy." I rubbed up and down his back. "Time to wake up." His sleepy eyes blinked repeatedly as he rolled to his back and stretched his arms above his head. "Did you decide to hang with Uncle Gavin last night?"

"Yeah," he said around a yawn, "but he farts in his sleep."

Suddenly wide awake, Gavin interjected, "I do not!"

"Do too."

"Do not! And *you* steal all the covers!"

Again, why doesn't my son want to play with other five-year-olds? He clearly lives with one already so it should be a no-brainer.

"Okay, okay, let's get up and leave Uncle Gavin to himself." I urged Rocco out of bed.

"What time is it anyway?" Gavin asked.

"It's only ten after seven. I had to get up early because I have something to do before work." I walked toward his door.

"Crap. Too early," he muttered, but I suddenly had an idea.

"Hey, since you're already awake, would you mind getting Rocco ready and giving him some breakfast? What time do you leave for work?"

"I'm working at the site up the street this morning. I don't need to be there till eight. I was *going* to take advantage and sleep in," he said pointedly. "Why do you need me to take care of Rock? Where are you going?"

Hmm, how should I handle this one? I didn't really want to tell Gavin that I was going to help some neighbors give his new company a hard time, but I didn't want to lie either. "Remember that lady who came by the other day with her kid? She wanted me to help her out with something this morning. I'll be back in plenty of time for you to make it to work." Vague, let's stick with that.

"Okay, I guess. Just give me ten more minutes of snooze time, Rock, and I'll get you some breakfast." Gavin laid his head back on his pillow and covered his eyes with his arm.

Knowing that Rocco can't tell time and Gavin, like me, possesses no internal alarm clock, I set a buzzer for ten minutes and turned the TV on to cartoons. "When that buzzer goes off, go get Uncle Gavin and tell him it's time to wake up. If he doesn't get up tell him that I will erase all his college women's volleyball recordings from the DVR," I told Rocco as he settled in on the couch. I may as well have been talking to myself. I paused the show and tried to block his view. "Tell him your clothes are lying on my bed, okay? I just need to run up the street for a few minutes but I'll be back in time to take you to school." I got a nod but his eyes never left the TV. I un-paused it and hoped for the best.

Wanting to stay in Charlotte's good graces but get this over with as soon as possible, I grabbed my cellphone and slipped out the side door, heading quickly toward the sidewalk. As I approached the end of our block where it intersected with Old Oak Ridge Road, I spotted Charlotte and Aiden with a couple I didn't recognize and a toddler girl who appeared to belong to them. The man also held a sleeping baby in his arms, wrapped in a pink blanket. Aiden was poking at the ground with what I hoped was a plastic knife, and he had what appeared to be an arsenal of various other knives tucked into some kind of utility belt looped around his pants.

Behind the group I spied two yellow construction vehicles—don't ask me what they were called—and a flatbed truck loaded with two more. The truck's signage read "Built by Murphy" and there were three men huddled in conversation to the side of the large vehicle—the tallest of whom held a cellphone to his ear with one hand, the other hand gripping the back of his neck as he alternately barked into the phone and to the men beside him. *Tense much?*

Charlotte spotted me immediately. "Hey, Laney! So glad you made it!" She waved excitedly.

I couldn't help but respond to her friendliness with a smile. "Morning, Charlotte!"

"This is Darcy and Glen. They live across the street from me, and this is their daughter Haley and this cute little bundle is Mackenzie." She gestured enthusiastically to each person in turn. "This is Laney. She just moved into Missy Greene's old place. She has a son who's only a year younger than Aiden."

After introductions were made and pleasantries exchanged, Charlotte got down to business and pointed discreetly to the group of men by the truck. The one who had been on the phone a moment ago was now scowling and gesturing angrily at a clip-board held by one of the other men. "Okay, so from what I know, I think one of those guys is the owner of the construction company. I figured he'd be the one to talk to." She looked back down the street toward our houses. "I was hopin' we'd have a few more people, but it looks like it's just us for now."

Little Mackenzie chose that moment to awaken and start fuss-ing. Glen began bobbing up and down doing the crying-baby-dance in what seemed to be a well-practiced routine. Charlotte looked at me. "Laney, you mind comin' over there with me?"

No, Charlotte, actually I think I'll just hang here with the baby and these people I don't know—you go on ahead—you see, my brother just started working for this company last week and it's the first real job he's ever had since he ruined his baseball career by being an idiot, and I kind of don't want to mess it up for him. But I'll be right here cheering you on. Go team!

"Sure."

There was absolutely no reason for these guys to think I even knew Gavin. I'd just keep my mouth shut and let Charlotte do all the talking. Piece of cake.

I followed Charlotte as she waved her hand in the air and walked toward the men, her auburn hair swinging and her hips sashaying in workout pants and a bright yellow fitted t-shirt. "Yoo-hoo. Gentlemen!" she called. I didn't know there were actual people who used the expression "yoo-hoo." I was loving this chick.

All three men turned in unison to the Southern firecracker that was Charlotte. The man on the left held the clipboard to his fore-head in order to shield his eyes from the sun, and his handsome face broke into a wide grin at the sight of my neighbor.

Oh, I knew this guy. Well, not this particular guy, but his type was unmistakable. He was the guy at every party, every gym, every concert with the cock-sure smile who stood a bit too close and made allusions to his cock size within your first conversation. He was also the guy who found any and every excuse to take his shirt off—*oh, is it hot in here or is it just me?* Gag.

My eyes moved on and I have no idea how the man on the right reacted to us because, as my eyes moved from cocky guy, they caught on angry-cellphone-guy in the middle of the group and chose to stay there for a nice long rest. *Thank you very much*, said my lady bits.

This guy was tall, he was built, he had a square jaw that could cut you, and despite the sunglasses that hid his eyes and the scowl that said, "don't even think about talking to me," he had my belly dropping to the ground in an instant. His almost black hair was in need of a cut and it looked like he'd been running his hand through it for a week. There was just the right amount of stubble covering his perfect jaw—enough so he looked sexy and a bit rough but not sloppy. My knees felt a little wobbly.

Paging Superman, I think I found your long lost, scruffier, sexier, and broodier twin. It was at this point I patted myself on the back for not wearing high heels because if I had, I would surely be kissing the dirt right about now.

Charlotte, seemingly right at home in the presence of hot super-heroes, kept right on going without pause. "Hello there. My name is Charlotte Baker. I live just up the street." She was already upon them and I scurried a bit to catch up. Charlotte looked back toward me. "This is another neighbor, Laney Mon—"

"Laney!" I interrupted loudly and thrust my hand out toward cocky guy. "Just Laney is fine." I avoided Charlotte's quizzical look. *No last names needed here, guys—let's keep it casual.*

"Well, Laney," I got the smile and nod as cocky guy shook my hand. "Charlotte." He switched to hers, handsome smile ready to charm our panties off. "I'm Mark. It's a pleasure to meet you both. This here is Doug." Mark indicated the man on the right whom I hadn't had a chance yet to assess. Doug appeared to be in his late forties with blondish hair and the beginnings of a paunch. Face unreadable, he nodded in greeting but didn't offer his hand. "And this is Nate. He runs the show around here." Mark turned his thumb toward the man giving me high blood pressure. Nate, face *completely* readable, turned his scowl on Mark, not pleased to be thrown under the bus. Unfazed, Mark continued, "What can we help you ladies with today?"

"Well," Charlotte began, her charming smile returning his, "I'm assumin' you're the company puttin' up the new property?"

When that got no response she continued, "Yes, well, we have some questions we wanted to ask if that's all right."

Mark, still the only one of the three to speak, moved closer (*See? I told you*) and said, "Sure. Happy to help." At this point I think it was safe to assume he was envisioning Charlotte naked.

"We've been tryin' to find out exactly what kind of business is goin' to be movin' into the new property. Can you tell us that by any chance?"

"Well, Charlotte," Mark began, "we won't really know that until the property is completed and the spaces are rented out, but I can tell you that there will be a total of three rental spaces. There are a variety of businesses that could make use of the spaces, but until rental agreements are signed, I'm afraid I can't be more specific than that. Wouldn't you say, Nate?" he passed the issue off, his eyes still glued to my neighbor.

"Yes Mark, I would say," the hottie ground out in displeasure, his voice low and a bit gravelly, perfectly matching the whole sexy, scruffy thing he had going on there. "Let's cut to the chase, girls, what is it *precisely* that you're concerned about?" His eyes moved to us, his impatience unmistakable. Somebody had a crap sandwich for breakfast this morning.

"Um," Charlotte was beginning to hesitate, "you see, we all have kids and we don't want to see any … *unsavory* types comin' around the neighborhood. And, um, increased traffic might be an issue too …"

"I see," Nate snapped. "So you don't want us bringing creepy assholes around your kids, and the tenants should stay off your street. Got it. Can we get back to work now? We've got a crew showing up in twenty and a long list of shit to get done. You can head back to your little mommy-and-me troop." He tilted his chin toward Darcy, Glen, and the kids. "We'll take it from here."

With that, he turned around and headed toward the cab of the truck. And, dammit to hell, I couldn't help but take in the view from the back with a little bit of "bow-chicka-wow-wow" echoing in my head. Thoroughly disgusted with my girl parts for turning to the dark side, I returned my gaze to Charlotte.

Her jaw hung open and she looked like she might cry. A surge of protectiveness washed over me and (mostly) overruled my baser feelings. She was a nice person—she didn't deserve to be yelled at by that, that big fat sexy jerk! She was friendly and cared about her kid and invited strangers like us to her house for playdates and just wanted to keep everybody safe! Sure, her son may or may not be a future serial killer, but everyone has flaws. What right did this guy have to berate her for asking a simple question? No way, you rude, arrogant, insulting, too tight t-shirt wearing *dickhead*—Laney Monroe has a bone to pick with you.

"Hey!" I yelled out to his retreating, sexy-as-hell back. "Nate, or whatever the hell your name is! You get back here and apologize to her. That was totally uncalled for!" My fists found purchase on my hips and I prepared for a fight.

"I'm sorry," Mark, looking not so cocky anymore, tried to interject, but the bell had rung on his bout. It was time for the heavyweight round. I shot him a look that silenced him, so I knew my message had been received.

Nate was back. "Lady, I don't have time for this. Doug has already told your friend by phone to contact the zoning board if you all have a problem. They permitted us to put this building here and as long as we follow all the rules set out by them, the city, and the inspector—which we will—this is *not my problem!*" He brought his face closer and ripped off his sunglasses, revealing brilliant blue eyes that were frosted over with disdain. "Look, it will probably end up being a nice little salon so you and all your friends can sit and get your nails done and have a little gossip session where you can talk shit about me all you want. *I don't care.* Now, if it's all right with you, I think I'll get back to work."

"What in the hell is going on here?!" came a loud and very, *very* familiar voice from behind me.

Well, shit.

I looked over my shoulder to find Gavin looking completely perplexed and Rocco riding on his shoulders, both hands grasping Gavin's ears like handles. But even the sight of my two guys couldn't stop the raging storm brewing in response to this absolute prick in front of me. It was *on*.

$\mathcal{N}$ATE

"I got this, Gav!" the ball of indignant fury in front of me called over her shoulder to—wait, wasn't that the new kid? *What was going on here?*

Why did I even bother getting out of bed this morning?

I should have known the day would be crap-tastic from the moment I woke up.

I'd accidentally left my phone, which doubles as my alarm clock, in the kitchen last night so I missed my alarm and, by default, my morning run. I need my morning run to clear my head and make a game plan for my day. I think better, feel better, and probably behave better if I get to run first thing.

And not only did I miss my alarm, I also missed half a dozen phone calls from work. The freaking siding we were supposed to install at the apartment project today had arrived late yesterday and nobody noticed until early this morning that it was the wrong kind.

Mark called first thing with that one. It was unclear if the error came from the manufacturer or from our end, which would make it even more complicated. But either way it left us with half a crew spending the day with their thumbs up their asses while we fell behind schedule and bled money. Not ideal.

I made a few more calls and we were able to shuffle some things around, but we were still going to be running behind until we got the right siding—and who the hell knew when that would be?

And behind all of that was the nagging fear that somebody would slip up and tell my father about it, which would bring on a whole new shitstorm coming from both him and my mom. Good Christ, I felt like chucking it all and catching the first flight back to Texas. This day was like screwing a skunk—it had hardly even started and I'd already had enough.

Mark, Doug, and I decided to touch base in person at the Old Oak Ridge site where Doug and I were planning on starting our day anyway. So, without time for coffee, breakfast, or my run, I'd taken the fastest shower known to man and headed over there. Suffice it to say, I was not in a receptive mood for any more bullshit when I'd arrived.

Enter the amateur pageant queen and her friend. Her smoking, fuck-hot friend with glossy dark hair halfway down to her ass and intense gray eyes that lit my dick on fire. Not to mention the rest of the package. To say I'm a tits-and-ass kind of guy is like saying the Cookie Monster has a vague fondness for sweets. And, *goddamn*, did this girl have some T and A. She had a little bit of that Christina Hendricks thing from *Mad Men* going on. And she was serving up the attitude to go with it. Maybe Texas was a bad idea after all.

I knew I was being a total dick, and I'm sure my hot little friend and her red-headed neighbor didn't deserve it, but I couldn't help myself. The crew was almost there and I had just gotten off the phone with the siding company—they were estimating another two weeks before they could get the right order in. That was a shit-ton of money and time, and I didn't have the patience to deal with these neighborhood people who were wasting my time with shit that wasn't even going to be an issue for months, if ever. So I released the asshole on them.

Sue me and then get me a coffee.

But it looked like this girl was just getting started, and now I was finding out she was somehow involved with one of my crew? What the fuck was going on with this day?

Her eyes blazed into mine as she drew in a deep breath in preparation for whatever was about to come. It was impossible to ignore the rise of her perfect breasts, and I caught just a glimpse of black lace at the vee of her red shirt from my elevated vantage point. It almost made me want to be cooperative. Almost.

"Listen here, you misogynistic prick."

Contrary to everything I'm sure I was expected to feel at that point, my dick rose to attention ("You called?").

"You can't stand here making your half-assed assumptions and treating us like we're some brainless little fairies flitting around all day with nothing better to do than take a crap on you and your macho-man bullshit."

Yup, still sporting wood.

"We are all homeowners on this street who have a right to know what is happening in our neighborhood."

She wagged her index finger in my face and I wanted to bite it.

"We take the safety of our children and families very seriously, as well as the value of our homes in which we have invested our hard-earned money—"

God, she was in my face now and I could see the dark ring around her flinty gray irises. Would they be the same shade when she was under me?

"Money we've made doing *real work* the same way you do, and I will not stand here and let you treat us like we are somehow less than you and your precious crew while you wave all your big muscles around and beat your chest!"

Big muscles? Now we were getting somewhere.

"Now," she commanded, "you will apologize to Charlotte for jumping down her throat and you will address our concerns in a tone that smacks a little less of arrogant dickhead."

If I didn't get her out of here I was either gonna kiss her or drop down on my knees and beg her to marry me. I had to find an exit strategy—fast.

"What did you say your name was again?" I asked.

"Laney." Her right hand suddenly rose and cradled her cheek.

"Your full name."

She swallowed. "Laney Monroe."

"Monroe." I felt the name on my tongue and kept my eyes glued to hers. "She belong to you, kid?" I yelled out to Gavin just so I could watch her eyes light up with rage again. God, this girl was smoking.

"I don't *belong to him!*" Her hand dropped and her voice

exploded with indignation. "God, you really are an asshole, aren't you?"

There was no arguing with that one.

With that, she turned and I got to watch the show as her perfect ass strutted away toward Gavin and the kid on his shoulders.

"Come on, Charlotte. We're done here!" To me, she shouted, "This is *not* over!" And all three of them headed out. I continued to watch the show, noticing Gavin glancing worriedly back at me a few times. He appeared to be arguing with her. With *Laney*. I couldn't blame him—that was the most fun I'd had in weeks.

Ten minutes later, with most of the crew in attendance I saw Gavin Monroe approaching, this time without the little kid and the hot girl.

"Nate, I am so sorry," he began. "My sister can be a little hot-headed sometimes but I talked to her and I promise she won't be bothering you anymore, I swear—"

"That's your *sister*?" I cut him off.

"I know, right. She's a pain in the ass."

I just nodded, not sure Gavin would appreciate anything I had to say about his sister's ass. "Don't worry about it," I threw back at him. "Go see Doug. We've gotta get things moving here."

And I would definitely need to carve out a little time in my schedule for a rematch with one Laney Monroe.

"No, Mark, my dad won't want to collect electric trains as his new hobby. And if you like your nuts where they are you'll mind your own business and tell Bailey to keep her gaping pie-hole shut from now on." I said to the moron on the other end of the line. Mark and I were pretty good friends but sometimes I seriously questioned his level of common sense.

It was Friday evening and I was standing on Gavin Monroe's front porch, having gotten his address from his employee file and hoping to catch his sister at home. I had yet to ring the bell when Mark called and I'd picked it up assuming, who knows why, that he was calling about actual work. Turns out Bailey had let him in on the search for Riordan Murphy's new hobby and he couldn't resist getting in on the action.

"Why not? I could get him one of those train engineer hats." He guffawed.

"Two things, Mark. One, you do know that even with a bum heart my dad could beat you into the ground, right? And two, don't even think of letting him or my mother get the barest wind of this conversation. The goal is to lower his blood pressure, not elevate it. And, besides, Bailey and I are family so he can't kill us. Just think about where that leaves you."

"You're no fun, man. I'm calling Bailey to swap ideas instead," he complained.

See? No common sense. "You go right ahead, man, but don't come crying to me when he turns you into a eunuch. Later, Mark."

"Later." He hung up and I turned to ring the doorbell.

However, the door was already open.

"If you're looking for Gavin, he's not here. He's probably at Jake's shooting pool. You should try there—I hear it's a pretty male-dominated crowd—hardly a woman in sight, so you should feel right at home." Laney gave me a fake-ass smile and started to close the door but I stopped it with my foot. Her expression changed to a glare.

"Whoa, hold on there. I'm actually here to see you." She didn't try to break my foot right away so I continued, "I wanted to apologize."

Her look turned suspicious. "Apologize?"

"Yes. You were right. I was an asshole."

"And have you directed this apology to Charlotte as well?" One hand went to her hip.

Oooh, she was a sharp one. "I will as soon as you give me her address. Can I come in before the neighbors start calling the cops?"

After a few moments she opened the door a touch. "I guess. But you have to act like a normal person. I have company and my son is here." Ah, so the little kid was *her* son, not Gavin's. But she didn't have a ring, I'd noted earlier. Still, I reminded myself to tread carefully. She stepped aside and left the door open for me. I followed her into the house and closed the door behind me. The doorknob fell off into my hand. *Huh?* I looked at her questioningly. She looked at my hand.

"Oh crap," she said and grabbed the knob from me while pushing the door to rest in a position that was mostly closed.

"You're worried about my building threatening your kid's safety and your front door doesn't even close?" I couldn't resist.

Her hand shot to my mouth and covered it. "I thought you were here to apologize," she hissed.

I was too distracted by the effect her touch had on me to respond. Her warm hand stayed over my mouth a few seconds too long as her eyes rose to meet mine.

Could she feel that too? Apparently so, because the next

second her hand dropped like it had been burned, and then both of her hands went to her cheeks and started running up and down over the sweet little freckles I'd just noticed. *Sweet little freckles? What was I now, a girl?*

She turned her back and hurried from the entryway. I couldn't do anything but follow.

It turns out we were headed into the kitchen where a very petite blond woman stood at a stove that was older than dirt, stirring something in a pot. The little boy from yesterday, who I now knew was Laney's son, was sitting at a blue table with a pile of Legos in front of him. He wore a gray t-shirt with a yellow chick on it and the words "Chicks Dig Me." Just under the sleeve of the shirt I could see one of those stick-on tattoos but I couldn't tell what it was supposed to be. I liked this kid already. I could work with this.

"Nate, this is my friend Fiona and my son, Rocco." Laney did the introductions, one hand still holding her cheek.

Oh shit, a thought suddenly occurred to me. Were these women a couple and this was their son? I was usually so good at spotting signals and I could have sworn Laney was into me, even if she didn't want to be.

The woman named Fiona whirled around, clearly not expecting a strange man to appear in the kitchen. She looked me over and I can tell you she was not shy about her head-to-toe perusal. I was beginning to feel a little violated, she was so thorough. Okay, so totally straight—that was a relief.

"Fiona, Rocco, this is Gavin's boss, Nate Murphy. Rocco, say hello to Mr. Murphy," Laney gently directed.

"Nate. Nate's fine. How's it going, Rocco?" I waved to the kid.

"Nice tattoo. Did you get that in prison? I'll bet it kills with the ladies."

Crickets.

"Five-year-olds don't really get sarcasm," said Fiona, leaning toward me and offering her hand.

"Oh," I said stupidly as I took it. Fiona couldn't have been more than about 5'4" and she was wearing sky-high heels, so her actual height was probably closer to an even five feet. She had light blond hair and a tiny face to match her tiny body. She was cute in a spunky kind of way, but was a complete contrast to her bombshell of a friend.

"So, Nate, I hear you've been stirring up some trouble in the neighborhood," Fiona led with a wink.

"Oh no," Laney interjected, "none of that. Nate is just here to apologize for yesterday and then he's going to be on his way." She had lost her slightly frazzled demeanor and was back in command.

"No!" Fiona argued and looked beseechingly at me. "You have to stay for dinner. I'm making penne with a fabulous tomato cream sauce and meatballs for my main man over there." She tipped her head toward the table where Rocco still hadn't acknowledged my presence and was busy building a Lego structure. "You'll love it!"

While the two women silently communicated in a series of indecipherable facial expressions and hand gestures, I accepted the invitation before it could be revoked. "Sounds great!"

"Are you the man with the construction trucks?" Rocco spoke his first words to me ten minutes later. We were all seated at the hideous blue table over bowls of admittedly delicious pasta. Fiona could *cook*.

"I am," I said, thrilled to finally have something that might win the kid over. I needed all the help I could get. "You like construction trucks?"

"Yeah. Uncle Gavin took me to see them yesterday but we only stayed for a minute. My favorite is the backhoe." All of his "s" sounds came out as "th" sounds and I had to admit it was pretty damn cute.

"That is a good one." I nodded at him.

He twitched his nose and went back to his meatball. It seemed I was dismissed. So much for that.

As Fiona had been preparing the pasta earlier, I took the opportunity to explain to Laney that my tirade yesterday had been the result of things that had nothing to do with her or her friend. I did a bit of light groveling and she seemed to be receptive on the condition that I also apologize to Charlotte. I agreed and the matter was closed. Why she chose to bring it up again over our nice dinner, then, was beyond me. I was just hoping that the presence of Fiona and Rocco would help keep things friendly.

"So Nate, you really don't have any idea what kinds of businesses will rent the space?" She licked some pasta sauce from her top lip and I had trouble concentrating on her question for a minute.

"Uh, not really at this point, Laney. I mean, certain types of businesses couldn't be licensed on this particular property anyway. There are rules for required distances from churches, schools, and what-not, but I can't really help you out too much with anything concrete." I brought another forkful of the delicious pasta to my mouth.

"But you'll own the property, right, so technically you can decide whether or not to rent it out to specific people, right?"

Oh no, we were not going there tonight. We were having a nice meal, her friend seemed to like me well enough, and her kid had even spoken to me. I was not messing this up.

I finished chewing and wiped my lips with a napkin. "There's actually a lot more that goes into those kinds of decisions. Is there any more of that garlic bread, Fiona?"

"Sure thing, Nate." Fiona handed me the bread basket. "I'm sure Nate's company will do its best, *Laney*. They don't want trouble any more than you do, isn't that right, Nate?" Fiona smiled at me and then let her eyes shift to Laney.

"Right," I responded and then shoved a whole piece of bread in my mouth so I wouldn't have to say another word.

"But let's just speak in hypotheticals," Laney continued, undaunted. It was like she was *trying* to annoy me. What was I saying? Of course she was trying to annoy me. "You wouldn't rent the space to, say, a medical practice, would you?"

Genuinely confused, I forced the bread down my throat in a painful lump and responded in a tight voice, "What's wrong with a medical practice? You could walk Rocco to a doctor's appointment." I gestured to the kid.

"I don't wanna go to the doctor!" Rocco objected vehemently.

"Nobody's going to the doctor," Fiona soothed him.

"Yeah, and some junkie would break in at night and raid the drug cabinet. That happens more than you realize," Laney declared, hand waving in the air.

I turned my head to the left and then to the right, looking for what? I had no clue. "What are you, a true crime author?"

"What's a junkie?" Rocco chimed in at the same time.

Sensing, as I was, that this was going nowhere good, Fiona interjected, "Time for dessert!"

Thankfully, the rest of the evening went smoothly. Fiona was very chatty, Laney tolerated my presence, and Rocco even spoke another handful of words to me. Laney and I exchanged a few more heated looks, hers possibly fueled more by annoyance than lust, but I'd take what I could get at this point. I had yet to get her alone again, though, so when it was time to leave I was thrilled that Fiona led Rocco down the back hall and Laney was left to walk me to the door.

"So, thanks for dinner," I said.

"Thank Fiona. She invited you." Laney tried to glare at me but instead I got a reluctant smile. Damn, she was pretty. Tonight she had her hair up in a messy ponytail and she was wearing a black t-shirt and cut-off jeans, neither of which could hide her curves. I was dying to kiss her, but I figured she'd probably slap me at this point.

As we approached the door I remembered the damn doorknob. "Laney, you can't go to sleep with your door like this," I told her.

She waved me off. "I know. It keeps falling off, but I can fix it. At least temporarily—until Gavin gets to it." She opened the door and I had no choice but to step out onto the porch.

"No offense to your brother, Laney, but he doesn't know shit about fixing things from what I've seen so far."

That earned me a bigger smile. "We'll figure it out."

"You know, I did notice a couple things in your kitchen that could use some attention too, and I've been told I'm pretty handy …"

"Handy or handsy?"

"Funny."

"I thought so."

"I've got some free time this weekend. I'd be happy to come over tomorrow and fix a few things. Truthfully, I've been spending so much time on the phone and driving from place to place that I haven't actually held a tool in weeks—it's killing me."

Oddly, she seemed to be holding back a laugh at first and ducked her chin to her chest. But then she raised her head back up, schooling her expression and starting to shake her head.

"That would be awesome!" Fiona's head popped in from out of nowhere. "She'll see you tomorrow morning." The door closed in my face.

"I'll be here at nine. I'll bring coffee!" I yelled through the door before turning around and stepping off the porch.

"She doesn't drink coffee!" came the voice through the door.

I smiled. I'd have to get creative then.

Chapter Eight
BOOM!

*L*ANEY

"Oh my God. When I turned around and saw that man I swear I ovulated on the spot. *Boom!* Instant fertility. They should give that guy out as a prescription—fertility clinics nationwide would fold overnight." Fiona looked at me dreamily and then switched to her mad face (which was ineffective on its best day). "Lucy, you got some 'splainin' to do—you did not accurately describe just how edible that guy is!" Her expression changed again as the wheels turned. "And did you see the way he was eye-fucking you across the table?" She fanned herself.

I put my hand over her mouth and looked over her shoulder. "Little ears, Fee!"

She peeled my hand off her face. "He's in the bathroom. I told him to brush his teeth so I could come back and eavesdrop."

"You know he's not brushing his teeth, right? He'll be back out here in three minutes wearing only his underwear and asking what he was supposed to be doing in there," I told her. "And Nate was not eye-fucking me! I can't believe you invited him over here tomorrow!" I whisper-yelled.

"Maybe I should open my own matchmaking business—it's coming back in style, you know. It could be Matched by Fiona." She motioned an imaginary sign in the air in front of her. "Kind of like Nate's company, Built by Murphy. It could be kind of a family thing." She gave a giggle.

"Fair warning—I may kill you. In the meantime, do I owe you a portion of my dowry now or will later be fine?"

"Later works for me."

A second dessert, one supervised round with the toothbrush, and three books later, Rocco was finally in bed and Fiona and I were relaxed on the couch with wine and girl talk.

"So, what happened to his dad?" Nate was still the topic at hand.

"Gavin said he had a heart attack a few weeks ago and Nate moved back to take over the family business until he recovers," I told her. "I heard Nate talking on the phone about trying to find relaxing things for his dad to do with his time. Sounds like a fairly long recovery."

"Oh my God," Fiona gushed and put a hand to her face as though I'd just handed her a puppy with a giant pink bow. "That is *so* sweet. He said he just moved back but I didn't know all of that. See? He's hot *and* he loves his family."

"Yeah, just what I've always wanted—a sexy man who loves

his family and hates women," I sniped. I was trying desperately to hold onto my mad but my resolve was fading. Evidently I was holding a puppy too, but mine had taken a roll in a pile of poo and still needed some work before it was as adorable as Fiona's.

Fiona swiped at my arm. "He doesn't hate women. So he was totally sexist yesterday—a real pig—but listen to *us*. We've been reducing him to a cut of brainless man meat for the last ten minutes! Face it—we *all* suck. But he apologized, didn't he? And he did seem genuinely interested in helping you." Her eyes sparked with a familiar shine. "And besides, did you see that ass? Like I said, '*Boom!*'" She did the fist-explosion thing.

"Stop. The last thing my ovaries need is encouragement to start sending out party invitations. Do I need to remind you what happened six years ago? And besides, you're missing an important point. *We* kept our sexist talk private—*he* broadcast his to all and sundry!"

"'*All and sundry*?' Are we in a Jane Austen novel now?" She set down her wine glass and sat upright on the couch. "I say, that gentleman's posterior looked positively fetching in those britches, don't you concur?"

I threw a couch pillow at her.

"Anyway," she continued. "It doesn't matter now because he's coming over tomorrow and there's nothing you can do about it. Can I come over and watch? I'll bring popcorn."

"Give me that pillow back. I need something to smother you with."

"Aww, I love you too, Laney."

A voice came from the kitchen. "There *is* a God. I think they're gonna kiss."

Fabulous, Gavin and his trusty side-kick were home.

"You know that's my sister, right?"

"She's not *my* sister," came the response from Brett, Gavin's best friend since high school. They both stood at the half wall watching us on the couch.

"Hi, Brett," Fiona and I chimed in unison. It's fun to play with dumb animals.

He may have whimpered a little while Gavin continued moving into the living room. "Who's coming over tomorrow?"

I arranged my face into what I hoped was an innocent look.

"Your hot new boss." Fiona threw my ass under the bus.

"No no no No NO," Gavin's voice escalated as he moved closer to me. "You promised me you were going to stay out of this! Jesus, Laney! You've spent the last two years nagging me to 'get over it' and I finally do exactly what you wanted and you start fucking it all up!"

"Be quiet! Rocco is sleeping!" I responded in only a slightly lower tone.

"*You* be quiet! I can't believe you! Call him back and tell him you made a terrible mistake and you and the mom squad are backing down for good. I actually like this job and I don't want to get fired before my first paycheck!"

"Get your damn feathers out of a twist, Donald Duck. Nobody's getting fired. I didn't even invite him over tomorrow. He invited himself."

"Well, technically I invited him." Fiona meekly raised her hand. We both ignored her.

"When exactly did this happen? How was it you and Nate were even talking to each other?"

"Listen, it's no big deal. He stopped by earlier to apologize for being a dick yesterday—" I held up my hand to keep him from interrupting. "And he noticed a few things that needed fixing so he offered to come by tomorrow to help out."

"Brett and I were going to fix things around here." His tone calmed slightly.

Fiona turned to Brett who had also entered the living room by that point. "I didn't know you were good with tools. How long has this been going on? I may need you to come over to my place and fix a few things."

Brett's upper lip appeared to be sweating.

"Since he was about thirteen, I think," Gavin said, all tension gone and a repressed smile replacing it. Hissy fit finished.

"Wow, that long?" Fiona replied.

"God*dammit*!" shouted Brett. He reached into his pocket and pulled out a wad of cash. He slapped a five-dollar bill into Gavin's already outstretched hand and stormed off to the kitchen. "Anybody want a beer?" he called out behind him.

If you haven't already guessed, I am in no way, shape, or form a "tidy" person. When I know company is coming over, I stuff everything in my bedroom or a closet. When I do laundry, only about thirty percent of it ever gets folded and finds its way to a dresser drawer. When I cook a meal, which I don't do as often as I should, I first need to wash the knife and cutting board because they are still sitting in the sink from last night's meal prep. Essentially, I was freaking the hell out the next morning in anticipation of Nate's arrival.

Expecting that he would probably want to check out the entire house, I was left with very few options for stashing my mess. Sure, he'd seen the kitchen and living room the night before, but I'd cleared those out before Fiona had arrived—although why I even bothered doing that for her anymore was beyond me. She was well aware of my cluttered and chaotic "decorating" style. When everyone was over last night, there had been no fewer than six pairs of Rocco's shoes crammed into the pantry, not to mention the unopened mail behind a potted plant and the giant pile of toys and clothes on my bed (or, more recently, my floor, since I'd shoved them all off before I went to sleep last night). So today I spent the entire morning alternately chugging Diet Coke and doing my best to make the house look like it didn't belong on an episode of *Hoarders*. A twinge of guilt almost penetrated when Rocco came out of his room and asked what was going on with his bed.

"I made it," I told him, assuming this was explanation enough.

"Huh?"

"You know, I tucked the sheets in the sides and arranged the comforter and pillow and stuff."

"I don't get it. They're just gonna get all pulled out when I go to bed tonight."

My kid was a genius.

"Exactly." I kissed him on the head just as the dying doorbell wailed.

Shit, poop, shit! I wasn't ready! I was all sweaty and I'm sure my hair was a disaster. I needed another shower after running around the house like an insane person. Well, too late now. Both hands rubbed at my cheeks.

Whatever. It wasn't like I wanted to impress him or anything. *Pshhh.*

I trailed Rocco to the front door like I was approaching my execution and watched him turn the finicky knob. And there, standing on my front porch, was my executioner—all six foot whatever of him in a threadbare t-shirt designed to render women speechless and send urgent signals right to their hoo-has. His shirt impeccably showcased his muscular chest and arms, and a pair of worn army green cargo pants showcased, well, all of *that*. And then there was the face, which looked even more flawless than it had yesterday, if that were possible—and next to the dazzlingly panty-melting smile sat one perfect dimple. The freaking puppy had had a full spa day. How the hell was I going to resist a fluffy puppy with not just a giant pink bow but a fucking dimple?

"Hey, Rocco. Laney." Nate pulled a box of Krispy Kreme doughnuts out from behind his back. Of course he did. My stomach joined my lady bits in celebration.

"Doughnuts!" Rocco squealed.

"Will this buy my entry?" Nate asked.

"Come on in, Nate." I stood aside and he handed the box of doughnuts to me. Hmm, apparently he didn't want any. He bent down and picked up a bag I hadn't noticed by his booted foot. I assumed it held his tools and supplies. He followed Rocco and me to the kitchen, closing the front door behind him.

"So you *did* fix it," he observed of the knob.

"Kind of." I twisted my mouth to the side, resigned to letting him have his way with my, um, house.

"I brought a replacement anyway. I hope you don't mind."

Rocco was already at the table stuffing his face with a doughnut, bits of glaze sticking to his cheeks and chin.

My kitchen was super cute, but I could see Nate's eyes assessing it the night before and I doubted he appreciated the awesomeness of my shabby chic table and my vintage fridge. I had to admit the linoleum needed to go, and in my dreams I'd get granite countertops and maybe even an island. But the kitchen as a whole was actually quite roomy, and nobody could argue against the big picture window that gave a primo view of the backyard. I'd dressed it in flowy white cotton curtains with turquoise tie-backs to match my table. I thought it looked amazing.

Rocco finished swallowing his last bite and spotted Nate's bag. "You got tools?"

"Sure do. I'm going to fix a few things for your mom. Maybe you can help me out." Nate leaned against the counter and crossed his arms over his chest. I checked my chin for drool.

Rocco looked to me and then back to Nate. "I don't know if I'd be comf-ter-ble with that." Nose twitch.

Nate looked a bit surprised and uncomfortable himself. I'm sure he had been anticipating drawing Rocco out with the offer of doughnuts and tools, but leave it to my kid to throw him for a loop.

"It's okay, buddy. You can do what you want," I told my son, knowing that pushing Rocco was never the best plan. "But can you thank Nate for the doughnuts and then go wash your hands and face in the bathroom?"

"Thank you for the doughnuts," he recited and then dashed off to the bathroom.

Nate and I stood facing each other in silence. He finally pushed off the counter and said, "So, you mind if I take a look around the place?"

"Help yourself. It's not big enough to require a tour so have at it." Fingers crossed he wouldn't open any closets.

He smiled for some reason and kept looking at me. Did I have something on my face? There was that dimple again and my lower belly started singing gospel hymns. He turned and headed for the hallway.

I craned my neck to watch him go far enough away before I pounced on the doughnut box and shoved half of a delicious treat in my mouth. Oh, yum.

A few minutes (and doughnuts) later, Nate returned. I discreetly ran a hand over my lips to hide any evidence and gave him my own smile. *Nothing to see here.*

He directed his thumb back toward the hall with an unreadable expression on his face. "Did you know your kid is in the bathroom singing about penises?"

Kill me now.

"Ah, 'The Wiener Song.' A perennial favorite." Gavin unexpectedly appeared behind Nate.

A bit startled, Nate turned to face him and then stuck out a hand. "Hey, Gavin. Good to see you, man." They exchanged macho pleasantries.

"Laney said you're gonna help her with a few things around the house. You don't really have to do that, man," Gavin told his boss.

"Oh, no, I'm happy to. I was telling your sister last night that I haven't gotten my hands dirty in weeks and I've got an itch for it." That wasn't precisely what he'd said. It seemed Fiona wasn't the only one dropping double entendre around here. *Oh please, you know you were thinking it too.*

"Okay, man, it's your funeral. I would stay and help you guys out but I'm supposed to meet my buddy at the gym." He hiked up his backpack over one shoulder. "Later." He passed by Nate, and before passing by me he discreetly pointed two fingers first to his eyes and then to mine. I flipped him off.

"What's that one for?" Despite his earlier reservations, it turned out Rocco could not resist the lure of power tools. As soon as the electric drill had uttered its first growl, Rocco was glued to Nate's side. I, on the other hand, was standing back but still enjoying the view and another Diet Coke.

"This is a Phillips head screwdriver." They were finishing installing the new knob and deadbolt on the front door. "You use it to screw in this kind of screw." He showed him the small screw in his hand.

"Can I hold it? What if you need to take a screw out? Do you use a different tool? Are there other ones named after people? There's a kid in my class named Philip."

Nate seemed a bit frazzled, no doubt trying to figure out how to answer four questions at once.

"I forgot to tell you." I approached. "Talking to Rocco is like attending a press conference. There will always be one more question."

He laughed and looked up from his position on the floor.

Damn, he was handsome. My hand itched to reach out and touch his hair.

"Redirection and distraction are your friends," I said. "And if all else fails, pulling a quarter out of his ear is a crowd-pleaser."

"Noted," he replied, still smiling, and went back to work on the door. "So, Laney, you never said last night—what is it you do for a living? I know you work in an office ..."

"Oh, right." I leaned against the wall next to the front door. I suck at small talk. "You know those new chips on credit cards that protect all your information?"

"Sure. I heard everyone was switching over to those. You program those?"

"No. But you know how some credit card machines still make you swipe instead of using the chip? Well, there are companies whose job it is to convert all the machines so everyone has to use the chip. That's what my company does."

"And you somehow make that happen?" He lowered the screwdriver again.

Rocco, clearly bored by the interruption in the action, wandered down the hallway away from us, probably to disrobe or make up a new song about vaginas.

"No. But I write technical procedures for the people who devise the *actual* procedures to make that happen." *Oh God, could I possibly be any more boring?*

"So, you're like the woman behind the curtain." It was sweet how he was trying to make me sound more interesting than I am.

"More like I'm the woman who transforms geek-speak into normal-person-speak."

He finished with the screwing (*ha!*) and stood to face me so I had to look up. His lips were curved upward and there was that damn dimple. "Ah, so you're a translator. That probably comes in handy in many areas," he mused. "Perhaps you could use your skills to help me understand women."

"No can do." I shook my head, feeling a little light-headed at his closeness. "Our jobs as women are to exist as enigmas whose sole purpose is to render men absolutely perplexed. Help me understand men, though, and I may be able to crack a bit of the code for you." *Oh crap, was I flirting?*

"That's easy—give us food, sleep, and sex and we're good." His lips quirked again.

"I'll jot that down." Mine returned the favor.

"Just be sure you reference the original source in the bibliography."

"Rest assured, I wouldn't dream of attributing that little gem of wisdom to anyone else. You are a true savant, Nate. Has anyone ever told you that?" *Definitely flirting.* This conversation was too inane to be anything else than a prelude to sexy time.

"Has anyone ever told you that you have a smart mouth?"

Before I could respond he tugged me into his arms and kissed the hell out of said mouth.

Bring on the sexy time.

Chapter Nine

FISHING

NATE

Her lips were velvety, and she tasted of mint and soda. One of my hands lifted to her cheek and the smooth skin I found helped me understand why she seemed to spend so much time stroking it herself. I could spend an entire day just kissing and caressing her lips and face alone—okay, well I doubt I'd be able to stop myself there. As my other hand reached to tangle in her hair, I tested the seam of her lips with my tongue and she parted without further encouragement, granting entrance to my tongue so it could taste hers.

I could feel her body shaking a bit, out of nerves or excitement I didn't know and I couldn't have cared less at that moment. But her tongue eagerly dueled with mine as I turned her toward the wall and pinned her there. My thigh found its way between hers and I pressed. My cock stood at attention as I ground into her leg with the finesse of a fifteen-year-old.

This girl was driving me crazy. I couldn't stop myself from bringing a hand from her cheek down her side and resting with my thumb just under her breast. She made a little gasping sound as she pulled her mouth away slightly to draw in a breath before moving back in for more. One of her hands drove into the back of my hair while something cold pressed into the small of my back.

Huh? Before I could comprehend what it could be it was gone and a loud clank came from behind me. Laney came to attention abruptly as she pulled back from me, a surprised look overtaking her eyes. The rest of her face remained flushed and her lips swollen from our kisses. She couldn't pull back far since I still had her pinned to the wall, and her breasts rose and fell as they remained pressed into my chest. She tried to look around me but my height prevented it.

"What's wrong?" I ground out, focused on getting my mouth back on hers.

"Um." One hand came to her cheek and her eyes darted away from mine. "I think I spilled my soda on you."

I stepped back from her and, sure enough, the can lay on the ground in a small puddle, and a hand to the ass of my jeans revealed a large wet spot.

"This is so embarrassing," Laney mumbled, still leaning against the wall, both hands to her cheeks now.

I couldn't help but smile at her. "Totally worth it."

She returned my smile, hers a bit smaller, then disappearing completely. "Shit. Rocco." Her eyes darted to the hall entrance.

Mine followed but no one was there. I admit I had completely forgotten about the kid, my attention had been focused solely on

Laney and getting my hands on her. In retrospect, I suppose my timing could have been better.

"I'm so sorry," she began again and darted around me toward the kitchen. "Let me get some paper towels and try to clean you, I mean *this*, I mean *you know*—up." She came back with the paper towels and tore a few sheets off, thrusting the rest of the roll at me. I wouldn't have minded her trying to clean me up herself.

"If you want, I can lend you some of Gavin's jeans and run yours through the washer," she offered from the floor where she was bent wiping up the mess. I had to force my gaze from her perfect backside.

"No thanks. I'll be fine." No way was I borrowing her brother's clothes. Just, no. "I've got to get going in a little bit anyway. I'll just swing by my place and change there. It's not far."

"I didn't realize you lived close by." She rose from the floor.

I could see her hardened nipples through her shirt and I lost focus for a moment.

"Yeah, I've got a little apartment between here and New Garden. It's pretty crappy, really, but it's just temporary so I don't mind."

An indecipherable look crossed her face. "Well, at least let me feed you or get you something to drink before you go. I can't let you work for free." Her smile was mostly back, some of her discomfort had dissipated.

"I won't say no to a soda, but this time you can just hand it to me." I followed her to the kitchen.

"Haha." Her cheeks began to pink again. Damn, that look was good on her.

I wanted to see how else I could get her to turn pink.

"I've got Diet Coke and Mountain Dew." She reached into the refrigerator.

"Mountain Dew. I've had enough Diet Coke already today," I teased again.

"You take classes on how to be a smartass?" The sass was back.

I took the soda and smiled at her. She seemed to like that because she just stared back at me for a silent beat.

Rocco skipped into the kitchen, ending our little moment, and a double take confirmed that, while he still wore the shirt from earlier, his pants were missing.

Laney's hand covered her eyes and then she shook it off and smiled at me. "Did I neglect to tell you we have a pants-optional policy in our house?" She seemed to realize exactly what she'd said a moment too late and I couldn't help bursting into laughter.

"Good God." She covered her eyes again but then smiled and threw a dish towel at me. "Shut up."

"You shouldn't say 'shut up,' Mommy," said Rocco, opening the pantry door. *Squeak.*

"I know, baby, I'm sorry. Nate was being very naughty and I forgot. I'm going to make you some lunch so we can head over to that playdate soon, okay?"

The kid didn't respond. But I noticed his nose twitch again. Did he have a troublesome booger or something?

"That sounds like fun," I offered, leaning against the counter and opening my soda.

Still no response.

"I'll bet you've got lots of new friends in the neighborhood, huh?"

Just a shoulder shrug and a nose twitch. Should I get him a tissue?

"I'm gonna play Ninja Turtles." And he was gone.

"Was it something I said?" I asked Laney, who had her head in the refrigerator pulling out lunch fixings.

"No, not at all. He's just having a rough time making friends his own age, and there have been a lot of changes recently so he needs time to catch up."

"Oh." I was a bit relieved to not be the cause of any upset. I was also curious about these changes but didn't want to pry too much. "So, I assume moving here was a recent change." I hedged.

"Very," she confirmed, now at the counter making a PB&J. "Until a few weeks ago we lived with my parents, but they decided to move to Virginia and it was time anyway, you know." She rested the knife and looked up at me.

No, I didn't know, but it was sounding like the baby-daddy wasn't in the picture. I wanted to know more but I stayed silent, hoping she'd elaborate on her own.

"It was great having all the help with Rocco, especially when he was a baby, but five years is a long time and it's nice to be on our own now." She looked around the mismatched kitchen with a smile. "I love it here." Her eyes landed on mine and must have seen the skeptical look on my face. "Don't start!" She pointed the jelly knife at me. "It has its flaws but it's just quirky."

"Well, I'm happy to help with those 'quirks' if you'll let me come back next Saturday," I offered, hoping she'd accept. The memory of that scorching kiss was urging me to push for sooner than next weekend, but maybe I should tread lightly.

Fuck it. "In the meantime, you could let me take you out to dinner."

"Oh." she set the knife down and, yup, the hand went to her cheek. Why did I find that so fucking appealing? "I don't know, Nate. You're Gavin's boss and ..."

"So, we'll leave him at home. He's a big boy and can get his own dinner." I tried to win her over with the smartass thing. That got a smile.

"Can I think about it?" she asked.

"I guess that's better than no. Let me give you my number so you can call me when you decide to say yes." Okay, a little cocky, but at least I'd get her number.

We exchanged numbers and she called Rocco in for lunch.

"You know, if you're so excited to hang out with me, you should come to this playdate with us," she said with a mischievous spark.

"Playdate?" I'm sure my expression was equal parts confused and apprehensive.

"Yeah." Her smirk was in full force. "The—what did you call it? Oh, right, the 'mommy-and-me troop' is getting together to strategize how to terrorize the big bad construction company."

My face completely fell. *Shit.*

"Oh, get that look off your face, Sparky. I'm just joking. You were getting too cocky and I had to knock you down a peg. I'm just going to tell them what you've told me so far, omitting the sarcasm of course, and explain that you'll do your best to keep us informed. I'll even try to convince them not to TP your trailer or leave flaming bags of dog poop on your steps. Happy?" Her smile was stunning. I had to get myself in check or I'd be hauling her off to her bedroom, kid or no kid.

Able to breathe normally again, I approached her and tugged on a stray lock of hair. "Not yet, but I'm getting there." Her cheeks colored again.

"Heh, dog poop!" Rocco chuckled from the table.

She lowered her face. "Let me walk you to the door."

I followed her after waving goodbye to Rocco.

"Wow! This works so well. I love it." Laney turned the new knob and swung the door open easily. "Thank you, Nate." She tilted her head to smile at me. Hell, if fixing her doorknob could inspire that look I could only imagine what other things could do.

We stood a bit awkwardly for a moment, looking at each other, both of us aware of how close Rocco was and how close we both were to saying, "screw it" and proceeding to, well, screw it. So I chose to bend down and kiss her cheek. "You're welcome. And don't forget to call me." She smiled but didn't respond so I turned around and stepped off the porch.

Halfway to my car she called out behind me, "Hey, Nate! Tell your dad to give fishing a try. It's relaxing while still being manly. And it involves both sharp things and motors—what's not to love?"

I did a half turn and pointed to her. "You just may have something there." I smiled. She certainly did have something.

Chapter Ten

WHEN IN DOUBT, CHOOSE BURGERS OVER SUSHI

*L*ANEY

Holy. Balls.

Nate Murphy has the power to make a woman forget her name. *How does he do that?* It's like his scruffy jaw and his dimple are my kryptonite. One moment we were having a nice little conversation and the next I had my tongue down his throat and was pouring my drink all over him. This was actually fortuitous since, in addition to forgetting my name, I had forgotten that my five-year-old was twenty feet away! I had been ready to tear my clothes off and beg him to take me right there by the front door. *What was wrong with me?*

Oh God, and then he asked me out!

Squee!

But not squee.

Shit.

There was Gavin's job and there was Rocco, and the last thing we needed was some guy who was only in town temporarily.

Ugh.

Not to mention it had been so long since my last date I'm pretty sure dinosaurs had still roamed the earth. I mean, a girl has needs and I'd been sort of satisfying them by myself for the most part. I'd dated a couple guys since Rocco was born, but nothing had stuck. And the fact I wasn't all that disappointed about it just went to show that those relationships were way wrong. But with the way I was reacting to Nate right from the start, I was pretty sure this guy had heartbreak written all over his too handsome, too freaking perfect face. And arms. And ass. Jesus, I was starting to sound like Fiona with all my scattered thoughts. *Get a grip, Laney.*

I had to set this incredibly sexy and tempting topic aside and focus on something else. Another date, in fact—the playdate. I peeled myself off the back of the door and headed back to Rocco. But I penciled in a good old-fashioned phone gab with Fiona on my mental calendar. I may have also penciled in a good old-fashioned fantasy session with my vibrator, but I'll never tell.

Charlotte's house was just as I'd imagined it to be—warm, comfortable, and wholly Southern. There were fresh flowers and sweet tea and, most importantly, welcoming hugs and greetings all around. Rocco suctioned himself to my leg but gradually loosened up as he saw some of the other kids organizing a few games. He eschewed the round of tag in the backyard—which, unsurprisingly, involved plastic knives and guns—and instead wandered over to check out the X-box battle that was launching in the next room. However, he made sure to maintain an open line of sight to me the entire time. I considered it a small win anyway.

Once I got a moment alone with Charlotte, I told her (mostly) about my visit with Nate on Friday and the information he'd shared. I explained to the best of my ability the cause of his rude behavior and told her he wanted to apologize to her. When I asked for her permission to pass on her number to him she graciously accepted, as I knew she would. It seemed all was already forgiven in her eyes and she turned them to me speculatively.

"So, do I sense a little chemistry goin' on here?"

"What? No, of course not!" I replied, totally unconvincing in my hasty denial.

She just smiled and raised her eyebrows. "Even if he was a class-A jerk, I'd have to be blind not to see the sparks lightin' up the air around you two." She was way too smug.

"Oh, shut up," I told her, and she just giggled. Damn her cute little ass.

My job was done. I'd shared my pertinent information, my kid was slightly engaged with others his own age, and I had a glass of real Texas sweet tea. *Ugh, why do people like this stuff?*

"Remind me. Why are you always over here when you could be out enjoying a totally awesome nightlife of hot guys and no responsibility?"

Instead of the phone call, Fiona had elected to come by my house for our girl gab. Seriously, she could be out doing anything she wanted at any time. She had money to party or go on vacations or buy out the entire SkyMall catalog—*hey, some of that stuff is cool*—but she chose to spend the majority of her time with me and my dysfunctional little family. To say she came from money was like saying Ghirardelli double fudge brownies were *kind of okay*. The bitch was loaded. Luckily, she was completely missing the "bitch" gene. She held rotating jobs mostly out of boredom and, I suspect, to generate stories to share with me when we got together. That's real friendship for you.

Truthfully, though, I don't think Fiona knew what she wanted to do with her life so it was easier to just keep busy and keep postponing life decisions. With her family's wealth, she didn't need to work if she didn't choose to.

In direct contrast to all the rich snob stereotypes, her parents were wonderful people who were in full support of any decisions Fiona made—and I mean *any* decisions. She could decide to move to some inner city to teach underprivileged kids, or tour Europe on a three-year luxury excursion, or tattoo her entire body and pose naked for a magazine spread. Nothing but love and acceptance would come her way. It was the simplest and most authentic relationship between parents and child I'd ever seen.

When Fiona was nine years old she'd received a death sentence in the form of an aggressive leukemia diagnosis. Through bottomless funds, prayers, and a wealth of medical miracles she had survived, and not only that, she'd thrived beyond basic remission and into adulthood as a healthy, happy, and wonderful person.

Sure, the aggressive treatments had resulted in her short stature and a slightly increased risk of developing a possible subsequent cancer during the course of her life, but she was our shining star.

Everyone who knew her and her sunny spirit reveled in it and called themselves lucky to know her.

Unfortunately for me, on this particular evening, the sunny spirit was hiding behind the complete exasperation in her expression.

"What?! It's just not a good idea. But believe me, I comprehend the sheer hotness of that man even more than you do. I swear there was a moment when he was kissing me that I thought I'd forgotten to put on underwear this morning."

She gave me a puzzled look. We both knew I was no commando girl. Not with my generous booty.

"I'd remembered all right—they had just spontaneously combusted under the force of his testosterone. Holy hell, he was that good!" I fanned myself at the memory.

We both giggled like idiots.

"Where are Rocco and Gavin?" she asked after we settled down.

"They went to the batting cages with Brett."

"Aww. That's so sweet."

Sometimes I forgot to appreciate the time Gavin spent with Rocco and the experiences he provided that a dad should be doing. It was time to lighten up on him.

"Yeah, unfortunately Rocco has a pretty un-athletic mother and a musician for a father so Gavin's dreams of living through Rocco may be dashed early on," I said.

Not to be deterred from the main topic of the evening, Fiona persisted, "So you're really not going to go out with Nate?"

"Ugh. Believe me, I'm totally tempted, but what happens when we get in a fight and Gavin gets stuck in the middle? Or, more likely, what happens when Rocco and I both fall in love with him and he takes off for his next adventure? Because he will, you know. As soon as his dad is back on his feet, he's gone. I can't do that to any of us. And even if, by some miracle, he decided to stay, why would he want to saddle himself with a single mom and a kid? I'm sure he's just looking for a fun distraction to pass the time and I'm not up for that." The feeling of sadness that overtook me was disproportionate to the brief involvement I'd had with Nate to this point. I could already feel myself getting in over my head and we'd only shared one kiss. One earth-shattering kiss, but still.

"But you deserve an awesome guy and a hot sexy love life, Laney! Every guy I suggest is all wrong—he's too short, he has a weird accent, he wears a fedora, he sweats too much—*whatever!* I can't sit around here and watch you spend another Saturday night watching *The Mentalist* on Hulu and fantasizing about Simon Baker—he's too old for you anyway. You need a real live date with a real live penis—your penis fly trap needs a snack! No offense."

Oh my, it seemed Fiona brought the big guns out tonight. "Wow, don't hold back on my account." I narrowed my eyes at her. "First of all, did you stop by a bar for a shot or seven of vodka on your way here? Second, you seem to have forgotten that one of the guys you tried to set me up with was eighteen years old—his voice hadn't even changed yet! Enough said."

Ready for her rebuttal, I thrust a hand out and intercepted it. "But, as it so happens, dear Fiona, Annette is setting me up on a date with someone this week. He fits all your criteria and he even has a child of his own. I didn't specifically ask if he has a real live penis but I'm assuming that's a given. I'm expecting his call and, barring a disastrous initial conversation, I plan to accept. So there!"

She beamed back at me and I couldn't help but be a little happy that I'd put a smile on her face. "Well, if it can't be hot construction dude, I guess we can give this other guy a chance at snack time. Now, where's the wine?"

My phone buzzed with a text.

Nate: I got an in at Hops and can skip the line. Just name the night. BTW, when did that place become such a madhouse? It's still just a burger joint, right?

Laney: I know! Ever since it got listed as "Best Burger" on some list you can't get in anymore.

Nate: I noticed that still wasn't a yes on the date?

Laney: I've got Charlotte's phone number for you.

Nate: I don't want to go out with Charlotte. I want to go out with you. Besides, dating married women requires too much effort and I'm not big on subterfuge.

Laney: Smartass. I meant I had her number for the apology you owe her. I haven't forgotten.

Nate: Neither have I. Now, about this date ...

Laney: I've got Rocco so it's not that easy.

Nate: You've also got Gavin and I am his boss after all. I can be lenient if he needs to come in late ...

Laney: Exactly! None of that. I don't think we should get involved.

Nate: You think too much.

That was Tuesday and I chose not to re-engage or I'd get myself in trouble. That same night I got the call I'd been expecting from Annette's guy, Alex. He seemed nice enough on the phone, although we did have the expected awkward moments one gets when trying to organize a date with a complete stranger. We settled fairly quickly on Thursday evening and I have to say I was somewhat relieved to get off the phone. I forgot how stressful dating was—why do people do this to themselves?

Thursday arrived before I was ready, and it was officially date night. The only problem was that the date wasn't with the guy I actually wanted, no matter what the logical part of my brain said. Nate had continued to text me since Tuesday and I couldn't help but be charmed by him. *Dammit!*

Determined to get me fired up for the date, Fiona showed up early in the evening with a slew of dresses and heels. Since she and I are nowhere in the neighborhood of the same size, my look of confusion must have been evident.

"So I stopped at a couple boutiques. Suck it!"

I would try to argue with her but there was no stopping Fiona and her credit card. So I let her spend the next hour doing my hair and makeup and dressing me up like a Barbie, except one with actual human dimensions. She spent the majority of the time alternating between reveling in her own genius and filling me in on useless gossip that was both totally frivolous and completely entertaining. As only a best friend would do, she'd offered to babysit Rocco during my date. I would have asked Gavin, but I was starting to feel like I was taking advantage of him a bit and I knew he had his, well, drinking or whatever to do in the evenings. Truthfully, I had no idea what he was up to these days.

"This is definitely the one." Fiona stood back and admired her work, finger to her lips.

I looked down at the form-fitting pink dress. It was sleeveless with wide straps—because, come on, there was no way on earth I could forego a bra—and a pencil skirt that ended just above the knee. Running down the center of the dress was a pretty little vertical ruffle of sorts. I tugged lightly at the ruffle. "You don't think this is too much?"

"It adds interest and draws the eye vertically—very slimming," she said.

I was all for slimming, but still. "You don't think I look a bit like … a vagina?"

She gasped just as the doorbell rang. "Shoes!" she shouted.

Oh well, too late. I shoved on the torture devices she threw at me and headed out to the living room. I paused as I noted for the umpteenth time this week that the cockeyed board on the hallway floor lay flat where it had once caused countless stubbed toes as if that had been its sole purpose on this earth. Nate had fixed it on Saturday and dammit if I didn't think of him every time I walked down the hall. *Sigh.* I forced thoughts of Nate aside and entered the living room where Gavin sat on the couch.

"Doorbell," he said oh-so-helpfully. Then he looked me up and down. "That's a lot of pink. No offense, but you kind of look like a—"

"You must be Alex!" Fiona opened the front door with a flourish.

I *knew* it! Crap! Too late now.

Alex stepped inside. Annette hadn't lied—he was super cute. Short-ish blond hair spiked up in artful disarray, and a thin nose held a pair of cool hipster glasses with black frames. He was taller than me in my heels so that was good, and he had great cheekbones, but no scruff, I noticed. Oh well. He wore a gray short-sleeved button down and black pants. Skinny pants. Huh. How did I feel about that?

Fiona swept to the side like the little hostess she is. She motioned to herself. "I'm Fiona, the best friend. That's Gavin, the brother." She spared Gavin the slightest gesture and then motioned to me as if presenting Alex to the queen. "And this … is Laney." Jesus, was she going to curtsey next?

Alex's face broke into a smile. "Wow, Laney, you look beautiful. I love pink."

Cough. Shut up, Gavin!

"Thanks. You look nice too." Didn't they have those pants in your size? I guess I'd figured out my feelings about the pants after all.

God, stop being a bitch, Laney!

He really did have a great smile—nice, even white teeth. But no dimple. Well that's okay, not everyone can have an awesome dimple.

Come on, give him a chance!

Fiona looked at me and seemed to be attempting to communicate the same command. *Let's do this!* "Well, have fun, kids!" she chirped and ushered us out the door.

The drive to the restaurant went as expected for a first date— some overly long silences and some talking over each other in an attempt to ease the awkwardness. Just normal first date stuff.

"I thought we'd try out this new sushi place," Alex said.

"Oh, okay." A bit of a risk for a first date, wasn't it? Not everybody likes sushi. *Shut up! You like sushi just fine.* "Sounds great!"

We arrived at the restaurant and he opened my door for me. Gotta love a guy with manners. He kept his hand on the small of my back all the way to our table which, while not prompting the flight of any butterflies, was nice.

After we were comfortably seated and had a chance to look over the menu, we placed our orders with the waitress. I stuck to the basics with California rolls, tuna and the like, but Alex went full out experimental. I couldn't pronounce most of what he ordered, and I was a bit scared to witness him eating it. Eek.

"So, Annette says you and Rocco just bought your house? That's great. Isn't house hunting fun?" he asked with a smirk. Sarcasm, I like it.

"Yeah, it comes in only a close second to a root canal on my list of favorite activities. But now that it's done I love it." I relaxed and sipped my water.

"I had to get a new place last year too. I thought my daughter, Allison, would have a hard time adjusting. Her mom stayed in our old place, you know, and we share custody."

I nodded understandingly.

"But Allison's been an angel—handling the divorce like a champ. Couldn't ask for a better kid."

That's sweet, I thought. I needed to give this guy a chance. "Wow, that's great for you. I've heard that can be really hard so it sounds like you lucked out." I smiled at him. "There's not even a divorce involved in my move and I think Rocco is going to need therapy to get over it," I joked.

"No luck about it. Allison's just the perfect kid." Deadpan.

Whoa, back it up there, mister. Isn't there some unwritten rule that you can't call your own kid perfect out loud unless you're using deep sarcasm? Before I had to think of a response our waitress came with our food and the hot sake we'd ordered. I think some of Alex's meal was still alive.

He picked up his chopsticks. "So, what do you like to do for fun, Laney?"

"Oh, you know, work and take care of my kid mostly. That's when I'm not flying off in my private jet to Aruba, of course." I popped a California roll in my mouth. Yum.

Alex shook his head and swallowed his bite. "You've got to make time for yourself. You should take up running. It's great cardio."

Was he calling me fat? "Running and I don't really mix." You can only get hit in the face with your own boobs so many times before you have to call it a day. "I like hiking, though, but it's hard to take a five-year-old. Rocco's ready to turn around thirty steps in," I tried to joke again.

"Allison loves hiking. We also do a lot of biking together."

I'm sure she does. And I'm sure your bike shorts are even tighter than your pants. "That sounds like fun for you guys." My appetite was quickly fading. I took a large sip of my sake instead.

"It is. She's really advanced for her age." He took a bite of what looked like a tentacle.

Of course she is. This date was officially over. Why did he need to date me when he had the perfect girl at home? "Well if I can get Rocco to sleep in his own bed by the time he's ten I'll count it as a win on my end," I ground out as I searched in vain for our waitress.

Completely misinterpreting my mood, he continued, "My ex and I employed a nurturing concept called the 'family bed.' Allison sleeps with me to this day."

Aaaand there's that. I was beginning to understand the cause of his divorce—and also the reason Allison was an only child.

"You should embrace Rocco's desire for closeness," he persisted.

I downed the rest of my sake.

Check, please.

"So it didn't go great?" Fiona asked, looking disappointed.

I don't know what gave it away, my scowl or my complete deflation onto the couch, vagina dress splayed around me. I was surprised to see Gavin in the recliner, leaning back in the same jeans and t-shirt he'd had on when I left. I thought he'd be three sheets to the wind by now at Jake's.

"Obviously," he contributed. "That guy was a douchecanoe."

I couldn't rally myself to protest. "Is it judgy of me to find it creepy that he prefers sleeping in the same bed as his seven-year-old?"

Fiona's expression crumpled with revulsion while Gavin's remained steady. "Dating that twatwaffle could only end in a smartphone full of dick pics. Consider it a bullet dodged and move on."

"Eww," Fiona and I simultaneously pronounced.

Chapter Eleven

WELL, THIS IS AWKWARD

*N*ATE

I hadn't given up. Several days of flirty texting but no date accepted, I still had my ace in the hole with a tentative Saturday plan to resume work on her house.

Nate: *Krispy Kreme again or should I go for Granny's?*

Laney: *Oooh. Tough choice. Surprise me.*

And just like that I had my confirmed invitation to come over tomorrow. It was Friday afternoon and I had to swing by my parents' house to get my dad's signature on a few documents. I hadn't seen him in about a week so I was looking forward to checking out his progress in person. My mom had told me over the phone that he was making her crazy trying to be too active and he was chomping at the bit to start driving again. That sounded about right.

She was also still on her kick to find him a hobby. Bailey had brought over a few jigsaw puzzles earlier in the week, as requested by our mom, and it had not gone over well. Some words were exchanged about nursing homes and bingo, and an alternative—and quite creative—suggestion was made as to where to put the puzzles. Bailey's visit didn't last long.

When I arrived, I let myself in the front door and was surprised to see that Bailey was back as well. Clearly a glutton for punishment.

"I thought you had an appointment this afternoon," I said.

"Canceled," she replied, chugging a coffee from Starbucks like it was her life's blood.

"Does Mom know you brought caffeine in the house?"

"I distracted her when I came in the door so I got away with it."

"How'd you do that?!" I had continued to get the pat down each time I entered the house.

"There he is!" exclaimed my mother, entering the hallway and consuming me in a giant hug. "My Nathan."

Looking over my mom's shoulder at Bailey, I spotted my conniving little sister's shit-eating grin instantly. She just shrugged her shoulders and mouthed, "Sucks to be you." I flipped her off immediately.

I was way too familiar with this look from Bailey. It was the same one she got each time she finagled her way out of trouble by throwing me under the bus. I'd spent many nights as a teenager, grounded in my room, plotting revenge on Bailey for just this kind of shit. It didn't matter that I actually *had* been smoking weed behind the garage or sneaking out my bedroom window to go out late—it was the principle of the thing. I'd been pretty successful with a few of my revenge strategies, the best one being the time I

THE FIX • 113

got the whole school to call her "Sabrina" for most of her freshman year. It was short for "Sabrina the Teenage Bitch" and the best part was that it could be used in front of teachers—it pissed Bailey off in the worst way. Ah, good times.

But that was then—this was now. And she would pay—as soon as I found out what the hell she'd done this time.

"Hi Mom," I said a bit warily, returning her hug with a tad less enthusiasm.

She released me and took my face in her hands. "So handsome."

Oh shit. This was worse than I thought.

"Now, tell me all about her. I can't wait to meet her! Bailey said she has a son. That's just wonderful! I miss being around kids."

Jesus H. Macy.

Skewering Bailey with my best "you are fucking dead" glare, I stopped her in her tracks as she attempted to slink away.

"Let's go have a drink in the kitchen and you can tell me all about her and her little boy," my mother cooed.

Trying desperately to get out of this conversation, I asked, "Where's Dad? I really need him to sign some papers."

She waved me off and ushered both Bailey and me toward the table. "He's in the shower. He'll be down in a bit and then you two can take care of that. Sit."

With little other choice, I sat and mentally planned my sister's very painful death. *Do they still have the rack?* No, that was too good for her.

Cups of decaf all around and the inquisition began. "Bailey said you met her at work? Is she Catholic? I'll bet she's Irish, isn't she? Oh, no matter—I'm sure she's wonderful either way." Her eyes passed between me and my sister.

At this point Bailey jumped in and tried to save herself. "That's just what Mark said. I don't really know much about it except for what he told me."

That bastard. Mark was too nosy for his own good and I should have known he couldn't keep his mouth shut. He had seen Laney at the Old Oak Ridge site, though, so there had been no avoiding talking about her. Every guy there had been talking about her for a week, much to Gavin's annoyance. Which only made the guys talk more shit, of course.

"Okay, slow down, Mom. I just met this girl and we haven't even gone out on a date, so hold off on the wedding plans, please."

"But you've been spending time with her, right? That sounds to me like dating. What's she like? I'm sure she's really pretty, isn't she?"

"Her name is Laney. She's beautiful." I couldn't help it—it just came out.

Bailey shot me a surprised glance, totally unused to me saying word one about a woman. Why did I feel like I was shooting myself in the foot?

"I knew it." Our mother smiled. "And how old is her son?"

"He's five, I think. His name is Rocco."

"Awww," came the two female voices simultaneously.

Jesus.

"I know!" My mother straightened up suddenly. "You should invite them over for Sunday dinner! Then we can all meet them. And it would be a great distraction for your father."

Before I could protest that nothing of the sort would be happening, Bailey cut in. "Not this again, Mom. A girlfriend or a potential grandkid is not going to keep Dad from going back to work. You've got to stop with this hobby thing too. You saw how he reacted to the puzzles. What's it going to be next, synchronized swimming?"

Bailey looked to me with a sudden smirk. "We'll have to add that to the list, Nate—can you imagine?" She started to snicker before she realized that she'd just fucked us both. *Have I mentioned what an utter pain in the ass my sister is?*

Our mother's good mood evaporated instantly, and the air turned thick. Her hands gripped her coffee cup so tightly her knuckles turned white. "So, you two think this is all a big joke," she said with a quiet intensity we'd never heard before. "You just wait until you see the person you love more than anything lying on the ground afraid and in pain. Then you see how funny it is to wrack your brain trying to think of any and every thing in your power you can do to keep them with you—to not lose them. Laugh all you want, but if puzzles or grandkids or *goddamned synchronized swimming* will keep your father with me for one more second, you better believe I'll pull out all the stops. Now, if you'll excuse me, I'm going to get your dad's medicines ready for him."

Imagine the shittiest you've ever felt in your life and multiply that by ten. That's how pathetic Bailey and I felt sitting at the kitchen table after the well-deserved beat-down served by our mother.

"God, we're such assholes," Bailey said.

"Yup." She'd hit the nail on the head.

"I'm going after her." Bailey rose from her chair and left the room.

I continued to sit and drown in the guilt. I had even lost my desire to punish Bailey, it was that bad.

Ten minutes later, Bailey poked her head in to tell me she was taking off and that she had apologized and tried to smooth things over with our mom.

Looked like it was my turn. I found her folding my dad's t-shirts in the laundry room.

"Mom, I really owe you and Dad an apology. Making fun of your efforts was cruel," I began. "I think … I think we were joking around and being assholes because we didn't want to acknowledge that maybe the strongest man we knew wasn't the superhero we'd always made him out to be. And even harder to imagine is *him* admitting that fact too. Sure he's human, but just because his heart wants to slow down doesn't mean he's not the same bad-ass ball buster and problem solver. But you're right—he needs to tone it down. And we need to be more cooperative in helping you accomplish what's best for you both."

She looked up at me and said, "I accept your apology, but next time, please try not to use so many curse words." She gave me a side hug and I kissed the top of her head, relieved to be forgiven. "This is hard on all of us—so many changes to consider," my mom said.

"Yeah, the changes are definitely throwing me. You know I'm all in with the company, right?"

"Of course. And you know we appreciate it so much, Nate."

In for a penny, in for a pound. "It's just that, ideally speaking, I would really love it if Dad comes back to take over the administration side of things and I can take over the other side. But I understand if it can't happen. I just want you to know I'm there for you either way, but I'd be lying if I said I didn't miss using my hands on the job."

She set the t-shirt she was holding on the pile. "Nathan, you and your father are different men. That's no secret to any of us. He's spent his career working out how to fit the figurative square peg in the round hole while you've spent yours *literally* fitting the peg to the hole. You don't need to become your father in some effort to rescue everyone. That can only end with you being unhappy and probably resenting us. And that is the last thing I want for any of us." She put her hand to my cheek. "We'll work it out. And I'll bet if you open your eyes and start looking around you'll see there are a lot of people who work with you and your father who'd be willing to step up a bit."

Well shit, why hadn't I thought of that? Why had I automatically assumed the bulk of the responsibility?

"So" she smiled at me and picked the shirt back up. "What time can I expect you all on Sunday?"

Aaand checkmate goes to my mother.

I'd decided on Granny's since I secretly loved jimmies—or "sprinkles" to the uneducated. The front door opened before I even had the chance to climb the first step, and Rocco burst onto the porch. "Is there chocolate?"

Ah, a man after my own heart. "Of course," I told him as if only a complete idiot would arrive without a chocolate doughnut. He snatched the box and ran inside.

"Rocco! Manners!" Laney appeared in the doorway.

"Oh yeah, thanks, Nate!" came the quickly receding voice muffled by what I assumed was a chocolate doughnut.

I paid zero attention to Rocco at that point, however. Laney stood before me in what I can only describe as the outfit that would have caused teenage Nate to sequester himself in his room for two straight weeks. The white tank top was thin, the pink lace bra playing peek-a-boo in several places, and her currently tightened nipples were straining the fabric. The tank was snug at her waist as well, and her hips flared out in a denim skirt which stopped mid-thigh. How I was going to get through this morning without putting my mouth on several parts of her body I had no idea. *Did she wear this fuck-hot outfit for me? She must have, right?* I was going with yes and pushing my luck as soon as the opportunity presented itself. With Rocco around, though, it was going to be a long morning working around the giant boner in my pants. How did this woman make me revert to a seventeen-year-old with one look and a tank top?

I stepped through the doorway and made sure to skim my hand over her waist and kiss her cheek. She smelled like coconut and a hint of flowers. Her sharp inhale did not go unnoticed. This was happening.

I spent the morning mildly flirting with Laney and placing casual touches on her arms and back as often as possible. Rocco resumed his position as my helper but lost interest a bit more quickly this time. When Gavin returned home from the gym and offered to take Rocco for pizza, the kid dashed out the door without a backward glance. Perfect. Alone time with Laney.

However, my normally confident air around women was a bit more elusive today, and I realized the reason with a mix of dread and uncertainty. My insensitivity with my mother yesterday had me consumed with guilt, and I knew I'd have to bite the bullet and embarrass the shit out of myself with Laney. I was going to ask a girl to meet my parents when she hadn't even agreed to go out on a date with me. Was there any way I could come across as more douchey or creepy than that?

Before I could stress any more about it, though, Laney walked into the bedroom with a basket of laundry and dumped it on her bed. "Can you tell me what the point is of folding laundry?" she asked.

"Um, I guess so you can find it later?" I didn't know how to answer. My wardrobe consisted solely of jeans, cargo pants, and crappy t-shirts, none of which required much care.

"I guess so." She sighed and sounded so disappointed I didn't understand how laundry could be such a downer.

"Is laundry really that depressing?" I asked as I finished gluing a floorboard in place.

She seemed to shake herself out of whatever mood had over-taken her and emitted a small laugh. "No, I guess I got stuck in my head for a minute there." She shook her head again and smiled at me. "So, what's it like working as my indentured servant on your days off?" she asked.

"Well, I'll tell you, working inside like this has its advantages. It's air-conditioned for one, and I don't have to hear passersby saying stupid things like, 'Hey, when you're finished there, why don't you come over to my house and fix a few things?!'" I mimicked an idiotic hillbilly tone complete with a fake-ass chuckle.

Her face fell. "I say that all the time … It's friendly."

She looked so disheartened I was without words for several moments. "Hmm, well, this is awkward." That's all I had.

We looked at each other silently for several beats. Then, finally, thank God, she broke out into the fucking cutest fit of giggles I've ever heard in my life. It was impossible not to respond with my own laughter, and pretty soon we were both doubled over. The situation may not have warranted the extent of our hilarity, but it felt so damn good to share this with her. I felt ten feet tall.

Since there's never an ideal time to humiliate yourself, I chose the moment right before I was leaving Laney's house. I gathered my things and walked into the kitchen where she was at the counter mixing something in a bowl. "Whatcha making?"

Her head turned to me and she had a bit of what looked like flour on her cheek. "Chocolate chip cookies. I figured if the doughnuts didn't put us into a diabetic coma this would finish the job." She smiled and turned back to her task.

I approached from behind and stuck my finger in the bowl. I got the dough to my mouth before she could smack my hand. "Psoo gwood."

"Hey! Taste-testing is only for the baker!"

I swallowed the pilfered bite. "It's just payment for today's work!" I then pressed myself into her back, forcing her closer to the counter. I could hear her breath catch. I leaned down close to her ear and whispered, "You have flour on your face," just to watch her raise her hand to her cheek in that way I found so endearing. I wasn't disappointed.

"Why didn't you say something sooner." She was flustered and started to squirm a bit which did nothing for the situation in my pants, considering my body was anchoring hers to the counter. I had no doubt she could feel my body's reaction to her, so I went in for a soft kiss under her ear. She melted into me a bit and I managed to turn her around so I could gain access to her mouth.

Our kisses were wet, hot, and fervent. Neither of us could get enough, and when my hand found its way to her breast she arched her back and pressed further into me. I rubbed her tight nipple with my thumb and she let out a small moan. My other hand caressed down her back and gripped her ass, pulling her in even tighter to my groin. It felt infinitely better than I'd imagined, and I'd spent a lot of time imagining it.

I was dying to get her out of this skirt and replace my hand with my mouth. Her arms wrapped around me and one of her hands descended to my ass as the other gripped my t-shirt. I was starting to lose control and was ready to prop her up on the counter and splay her out. I knew I had to slow down or I'd scare her away for sure. I pulled back reluctantly with one last squeeze of her ass and we both breathed deeply. She raised her hand again, but this time it was to touch her lips which were swollen from our kisses.

"You still think it's a bad idea to go out with me?" I asked.

She smiled and her cheeks remained pink as we both continued to steady our breaths

"I'll tell you what," I said, my hand caressing up and down her side. "You don't even have to be alone with me for our first date. As strange as it sounds, I'd like to ask you and Rocco to come over for dinner at my parents' house tomorrow." I held my breath and hoped for the best.

A perplexed look crossed her face. "I'm sorry, did you just ask me to meet your parents tomorrow?"

"It's not what it sounds like. My mom's a terrible cook but she wants to have people over to hang out with my dad and I have trouble saying no to her. Don't overthink it—just say yes."

"Um, okay then, I guess we can come." Then she quickly added, "Can I bring Gavin?" It seemed she wanted to make sure this wasn't a date. As long as she was coming, though, I didn't care who she brought with her.

"Sure. The more the merrier. That way we'll have more people to hang out with at the hospital when we all get food poisoning."

Her face fell.

"Kidding. But, seriously, you may want to eat before you come."

I offered to pick her up but she assured me they could get there on their own, so once I gave her the address it was time for me to leave. We walked to the door together and I couldn't help but pull her to me for one more short kiss. She tasted like cookies.

"I'll call you later," I said and walked to my truck, afraid if I didn't leave now I never would.

Once I got to my car I called Bailey and told her the Monroe troop was coming tomorrow and she'd better get her ass on the phone and invite someone too—in order to keep things as casual as possible. I could tell right away she was going to try to bail, so like any good brother would, I employed blackmail to get my point across.

"Oh, did I forget to tell you I gave Vance your number?" Vance was the creepy electrician we contracted with on occasion, and he had a serious thing for Bailey. "I said you would be waiting for his call and were really looking forward to getting to know him better. I think he mentioned dinner at his place—I can't recall all the details, but I'm sure it won't involve any lotion on the skin or anything."

"I hope you choke on your own dick. You didn't actually do that, did you?"

"Not yet, but I do have his number on speed dial."

"Fuck you. What time do we have to be there?"

Chapter Twelve

WE'VE ALL GOT OUR OWN BRAND OF CRAZY

*L*ANEY

"I got an email today that I know was from you, but the sender was 'Mommy Buttlover'? What the fuck?" That was Fiona's greeting when I called her to fret about Nate that afternoon. She was trying not to laugh and doing a piss-poor job at it.

"Christ on a cracker—I know. I'm going to *kill* Gavin. No one will recognize his body. He had Rocco tell Siri to call me 'Mommy Buttlover' from now on instead of 'Laney,' and it changed my outgoing email identifier! I replied to just about everyone in my address book today about a birth announcement. Everyone is going to see that 'Mommy Buttlover' thinks the baby looks just like his daddy. God, how embarrassing!"

"Not to mention confusing." She was cackling by this point and I couldn't help but smile a tiny bit.

"I hate my life," I managed.

"No you don't. Your life is great—awesome kid, cute house, sadistic brother … what more could you ask for? Except maybe … hot construction guy?" I could see I wouldn't have to introduce the real reason for the call. She knew me too well.

"I'm starting to think hot construction guy is going to be a part of my life whether I want him to be or not."

"I knew it, I knew it," she sing-songed loudly in my ear.

"We totally made out again in my kitchen and he asked me to have dinner with his parents tomorrow," I blurted out.

Silence.

"It's weird, isn't it?" I stated more than asked.

"Well, the making out part isn't weird at all—in fact, that part is dreamy—and please tell me you got to touch his butt and it was as perfect as it looks."

"Yes, and *hell yes*."

"I knew it!" The song was back.

"Okay, shut up. The make-out session was so hot I can't even begin to describe it accurately. My breasts physically swelled—I didn't even know that could happen. But the dinner thing is stressing me out!"

"All right, calm down. How exactly did he ask you? Was he like, 'Hey, Laney, since we made out a couple times and we're clearly getting married why don't you come meet Mom and Dad tomorrow and then we can make beautiful babies together?' or was it more like, 'Hey, I'm going over to my parents' to grab a bite. Wanna come?'"

"I guess it was more like the second one. He invited Rocco and Gavin too."

"Then what are you stressing about? I think it's sweet."

"You do? You're sure?"

"Yeah. You worry too much. Go and have fun and then report back to me. Now get back to Nate's ass—I need more details!"

"Why is it we never talk about your love life?"

After the whole Siri debacle, it wasn't too hard to guilt Gavin into coming to dinner at the Murphy's. It did involve free food, after all, but I neglected to warn him about Mrs. Murphy's supposedly horrific cooking. *Can you blame me?* I fed Rocco a sandwich before we left so he would be all set—Gavin could fend for himself.

I was a little distracted on the drive over. Charlotte and I had met up that morning at a nearby park and I'd been hoping Rocco would play with Aiden, but he mostly just asked me to swing him on the swings while Aiden ran around shooting imaginary villains and mounting attacks from the top of the monkey bars. Charlotte and I had a nice time talking and I was liking her more and more— now if I could only get our kids to be friends.

Feeling a bit down from the park, I'd called my mom to catch up and see if she could offer me some reassurance. She was aware of Rocco's little idiosyncrasies, having lived with him since his birth. I filled her in about the nose thing and his recent behavior.

"I feel like it's getting worse since we moved to the new house." I didn't want to say, "since you moved away" because it was definitely not her cross to bear—she'd gone above and beyond as a grandparent. "And now his teachers are concerned."

"Sweetie, all moms worry about their kids. Rocco's not even

going into real school until next year—a lot can change in a year. And might I remind you of another person in our family who has a little habit of her own—someone who rubs her face when she's stressed?"

Oh yeah, why didn't I think of that? Well, poop, it looked like I'd passed down more of my own issues to the poor kid than I realized.

"And, besides, kids are just small adults—have you ever met an adult who was normal? Of course not. We all have our own brand of crazy. Just love him and that's all you can do," she said.

"I just can't help but feel like *I've* done this to him. *I* deprived him of a father by being irresponsible and *I* moved him away from people he loves. And now it looks like *I* gave him a tic for God's sake!" It felt both good and awful to say it out loud.

"Laney, all parents second-guess themselves and feel 'less than' at times. And we *all* make mistakes. I've never told anyone this, but I dropped your brother on his head when he was about two months old—smack on top of his soft little head!"

"I know."

"How do you know that? Even your dad doesn't know that."

"Well, it's a more believable explanation than the possibility that you experimented with drugs while pregnant with the idiot."

See? I knew my mom could make me feel a bit better.

Now we were on our way to the Murphy's, and I tried to put my worries about Rocco out of my head and instead focus on (i.e. worry about) the evening ahead. At this rate, I'd have an ulcer by next week. Couldn't wait.

"I'm still confused about how I got talked into this," Gavin said from the driver's seat of his beat-up Jeep. I never argued when

Gavin wanted to drive because he is the world's absolute worst backseat driver. I was honestly more likely to run into a tree with Gavin in my car than I would be had I been a blind person.

"Will they have cookies?" Rocco asked from the back seat where he was taking apart a Transformer.

"I don't know, sweetie. Mr. Murphy is on a special diet and I don't think he's allowed to have cookies."

"But I'm not on a special diet," he answered as only a kid can.

"Don't worry, Rock, we'll get you one of your mom's cookies when we get home," Gavin reassured, never one to deny my kid something sweet.

"You know, Gav. You should be happy I talked you into this. It could be a boost for your career," I teased. "It'll give you a chance to suck up to not just the boss but the *big* boss."

"Haha. I don't want to look like a douche."

"What's a douche?" Rocco asked.

I gave Gavin the evil eye. "It's just an adult thing, Rocco. You should never say that word."

"But what is it?"

"It's a special kind of soap for adults," answered Gavin, never understanding that in a kid's hands, too much knowledge is too much power.

"No, Rock, it's a bad word some adults say. Just ignore your uncle."

Gavin came back to the original topic. "I don't want to suck up —I'm just gonna stay quiet while Nate spends the evening checking you out." An overly dramatic shiver coursed through his body. "I can't believe you're dating my boss."

"I'm not dating him! And this is definitely not the time to talk about this." I motioned to the listening ears in the booster seat behind us.

"Whatever. I know what's going on even if you don't. All I have to say is you'd better not mess this up for me, Laney," he warned.

"I'm not messing anything up. We're just having dinner at their house."

"Said the most clueless human on the planet. Oh, and just make sure to keep it wrapped this time around." I had to slap him even if he was driving at the time.

We arrived ten minutes later at a beautiful two-story brick home in an elegant community with big, lush lawns and gorgeous crepe myrtles dotting the tree-lawn all along the street. Rocco and I got out first and headed to the door while Gavin grabbed some things I'd brought along from the back. I carried a bouquet of flowers as well as a tin of heart-friendly muffins I'd baked for Nate's dad, and I let Rocco ring the bell. The door immediately opened and there was Nate in all his perfect scruffy handsomeness. *Sigh.* He wore another pair of faded jeans and a vintage Rolling Stones t-shirt, his hair looking like he'd been running his hand through it. Maybe he was nervous too.

"You made it," he greeted and leaned over to place a hand on my waist and a light kiss on my cheek. "Come in." He moved to the side to allow us entry. "Hey Rocco, how's it going?" Rocco just gave a silent little wave accompanied by a nose twitch and stuck to my side.

Nate seemed to let it roll off his back. "My mom is in the kitchen doing some last-minute stuff or she would have greeted you herself."

"Oh, I totally understand. No problem. Gavin's just grabbing some things from the car—he'll be here in a minute." My nerves were eating at my stomach as Nate led us into a living room and invited us to take a seat. I remained standing and I could hear some banging coming from the kitchen. "Are you sure I can't help your mom with something?"

Nate looked unsure. Then a loud curse rang from the kitchen. "Uh, maybe we should." I followed him, flowers and muffin tin in hand.

"Rocco, go help Uncle Gavin bring the things in from the Jeep, okay? I'll just be right in the kitchen." And that's when I got my first glimpse of Mr. and Mrs. Murphy. He was bent over looking into the open oven and cursing a blue streak while she was slapping at a burning dish towel with a spatula.

"Mom!" Nate exclaimed and grabbed the towel from her hand, throwing it directly into the sink and turning the tap on.

"I just asked if it was overcooking! I didn't tell you to light your damn self on fire!" came the gravelly voice from over by the oven.

"I was trying to pull it out. It's not my fault the towel caught on the heating element! Nate, can you pull the chicken out of the oven for me?" asked Mrs. Murphy, blowing her swath of blond hair from her eyes and peering into the sink at the smoking towel.

"I'm not a cripple, Erin! For Christ's sake, I can lift a damn pan from the oven."

"Not yet, you can't—not until the doctor okays it."

"Nate, hand me that towel. No, the other one. I'm pulling this thing out before your mother burns the house down."

Nate shot me a look that said he regretted inviting me over

more than anything he'd ever done in his entire life. I just sent him the brightest smile I had. Oddly, the chaos in the room served to calm my nerves completely. Turns out my mom was right—everybody does have their own brand of crazy. And the Murphys' brand involved yelling and spazzing out and cussing, and I couldn't have felt more at home.

"Uh, Mom, Dad, this is Laney." Two heads swung simultaneously to me.

"Oh my word. Laney." Mrs. Murphy brought one hand to her hair and the other to her ample hip. "You must think we're insane. I am *so* sorry!"

"Not at all," I laughed. "It actually reminds me of home. It's lovely to meet you, Mrs. Murphy. Oh, and I brought these for you." I extended the flowers and muffins.

She came over, grabbed the offerings and shoved them in Nate's hands and then proceeded to envelop me in a full-body hug the likes of which I'd never experienced before. "Call me Erin." In that moment I think I missed my mom more than I'd realized. "And thank you for the gorgeous flowers and whatever's in that tin—I'm sure it will be delicious," she said, still hugging me.

The sound of the doorbell caused her to finally release me, and she turned toward the foyer.

"That'll be Laney's son and her brother," Nate explained as Erin hurried off to answer the door.

"So, Laney," Mr. Murphy began. He was just as tall as Nate and I could immediately spot the resemblance. They shared the same blue eyes, and although the older man's hair was peppered with gray and he carried some extra weight, the similarities were undeniable. "I hear you've been spending some time with my son. I hope he's treating you right."

"He's a perfect gentleman." *Well, most of the time.* "He's helping me out a lot around my house. Thanks to him my doorbell no longer sounds like a drowning cat and I don't trip over my uneven floor on my way to the kitchen anymore."

"Good, well you just let me know if he steps out of line and I'll straighten him right up." He smiled at me, and wouldn't you know it, there was an identical copy of that damn dimple.

Nate just rolled his eyes at his dad. "You're looking good, old man, but I still think I could take you."

"Yeah, you just try," he responded, the affection between the two obvious.

It was then that Rocco bounded into the kitchen followed by Gavin, who wore an indiscernible expression. He approached Nate and said quietly, "Dude. I don't want to alarm you, but your mom just groped me in the entryway. I think I might be pregnant."

Nate snickered. "Ah, the pat-down. She was just checking for contraband. Don't worry—your virtue is safe."

I didn't even want to know what that was about, so when Erin re-entered the kitchen I quickly made introductions. Rocco was shy, as usual, and I noticed a few nose wiggles, but with three familiar adults in the room and Erin's innate warmness, he was soon emerging from his shell a bit.

The surprise of the evening, though, was how taken Rocco was with Nate's dad, whose name I learned was Riordan. The older man held a seemingly endless store of kid-friendly jokes and he soon had Rocco in fits of giggles. I couldn't help it when my eyes teared up a bit. Nate immediately noticed and laid a hand on the small of my back, not removing it until his sister, Bailey, arrived with a friend and we all sat down for dinner. Nate's arm then moved to the back of my chair and remained there throughout the entire meal.

Erin had set the flowers I brought as the centerpiece to the table and she thanked me profusely for the muffins I'd made using applesauce instead of butter. Who knew how they'd taste, but it was worth the effort.

Conversation over dinner was lively, and I couldn't remember laughing so much in a very long time. The company definitely made up for the almost inedible chicken, and one look around the table showed all parties' creative attempts at hiding their uneaten chicken on their plates. Thankfully Rocco didn't blurt out any embarrassing comments about the food. Instead he just stuffed his face with rolls and exchanged more jokes with Riordan. Within the flow of conversation around us, I noticed Bailey not so subtly checking me out throughout dinner. But with Nate's regular grazes of my shoulder and neck, I maintained my composure and just tried to smile back at her.

I could see some resemblances between Bailey and the rest of her family. She shared Nate and Riordan's blue eyes, but her hair had clearly come from Erin. It was a beautiful shade of blond and she wore it in a ponytail with a big swath of bangs angled across her forehead. She was also fairly tall—I'd guess maybe 5'7"—which was no surprise considering the height of her brother, and she seemed to share my preference for casual clothes.

While Bailey conversed naturally with everyone throughout the meal and entertained us with some stories (as well as some incredibly well-timed insults at Nate's expense), her friend Kia was less than entertaining. She chattered like a sixteen-year-old girl on a caffeine drip and seemed not to realize that none of her stories were hitting the mark. We were all too polite to let it show, of course, responding instead with head nods followed by a change in subject. I caught Nate shooting looks at Bailey every once in a while, which she responded to with wide smiles. It was after a particularly mind-numbing tale of a nail appointment gone wrong that Gavin decided he was done being polite. Why he thought it was a good idea to provoke a confrontation at his boss's dinner table I have no idea, but as I've stated before, Gavin is an idiot.

"Hey, Kia, do you by any chance have an off button, or maybe just a pause button. My head is about to explode."

I was completely mortified. Kia's jaw hit the table in indignant shock. Erin covered her mouth with a napkin that hid what I thought might have been a smile. Riordan stole another roll. Nate and Bailey shared a look across the table and then simultaneously burst out into gales of laughter.

Assholes!! What was going on here?

"You." I pointed at Nate. "Hallway." I stood, and to the rest of the table I simply said, "If you could excuse us for a moment, we'll be right back." I could see Erin smacking Bailey on the arm and Kia standing up in a huff to gather her purse. Gavin sat back with a smirk, too damn cocky to consider he could have just blown his professional reputation. *Ugh!*

Riordan and Rocco went back to business. "Stop me if you've heard this one. A guy with a peg leg walks into a bar—"

"What's a peg leg?"

In the hall, Nate was ready for me and was already defending himself before I could draw in a breath. "Look, you have to understand Bailey. We live to torture each other and when I told her she had to invite someone to dinner to make you feel more comfortable she decided to choose the most annoying person on her contact list. I should have seen it coming but I was so nervous about not freaking you out and about getting this evening to go well, I completely missed the opening I'd given her. It's my fault, but I promise everyone in there, with the exception of Kita or Kia or whoever, thought that whole scene was fucking hilarious."

What was I going to do with him? Having no answer I decided to settle for punching him in the arm. He laughed and pulled me into a hug.

After many thank-yous and another round of hugs goodbye we all headed to the front door. Riordan opted to stay in the kitchen to wash dishes, but he fist-bumped Rocco goodbye and gave us all a wave.

"What is all of this?" Erin said as we approached the front door and she saw a couple boxes and a tall cylindrical case leaning against the wall.

I bit my lip. "I didn't want to be presumptuous, but I had all this fishing equipment from my parents' house that I was planning on using with Rocco. We haven't had the time and it's just been gathering dust so I thought maybe Riordan might be interested in trying his hand at it. There are some great ponds and reservoirs around here. It's probably stupid, but I used to love to fish with my dad and he always said it was one of life's best pastimes. Like I said, it's a silly idea but if you're interested feel free to use it," I finished, suddenly feeling shy.

Erin wrapped me in another enormous hug and whispered in my ear, "You're an angel, Laney." I guess it wasn't such a silly idea after all.

On the front walkway Bailey stopped me. "Sorry if that whole Kia thing made you uncomfortable. I was so focused on annoying Nate I didn't really think about making it weird for you. Honestly, that girl has had the biggest lady boner for Nate for so long I'm actually relieved I brought her here tonight. Hopefully she'll leave me alone about it now that she sees he's officially taken," she said.

I had no response. Luckily, she seemed to not need one as she waved and jogged to her car.

Nate walked the rest of us to the Jeep. He opened the passenger door for Rocco and me. Before he closed it, he leaned down toward me. "Text me so I know you got home safe."

All signs indicated Laney Monroe had just gotten herself a boyfriend.

Eek!

Chapter Thirteen

IT'S A GRAY AREA

NATE

Nate: *So what night is best for you this week?*

Laney: *For what?*

Nate: *For our second date?*

Laney: *When did I agree to our first date?*

Nate: *It was implied. You had dinner with my parents and a psychotic person. I really should count that as two dates.*

Laney: *Ha.*

Nate: *Just so you know, Gavin is available to babysit on Wed or Thurs.*

Laney: *You're involving my brother in this? That's extortion— you're his boss.*

Nate: *It's a gray area. How about Wednesday? I'll cook for you. Don't worry, I didn't learn from my mom.*

Nate: *I'm getting gray hair over here waiting.*

Laney: *Wednesday. I can be ready at 6:30.*

Nate: I'll pick you up. Later, Laney.

Laney sure knew how to get under my skin. Not to be cocky, but I knew she was into me, so I couldn't figure out the reluctance on her part. I'd never had to work so hard to get a girl to date me, and there had never been a girl I was so eager to date before. She did things to me I couldn't explain. I must have replayed our two kisses in my head a hundred times, many of those times occurring in the shower with my hand in full participation, I am not ashamed to say. I also found myself thinking of her at the oddest times—like when I went to the grocery store and saw some chocolate chip cookies, it reminded me of the ones she'd made (and the kiss involved). Or when I picked up some supplies at Home Depot, I bought a flashlight because I'd noticed Laney didn't seem to have one. This girl was firmly rooted in my head.

Maybe the reluctance on her part was because of Rocco—I suppose that made sense. I'd never dated a single mom before, and it was bound to be more complicated. I confess I don't know the first thing about kids, but I like them well enough. I'd just never had the chance to spend a lot of time with them. Rocco seemed like a cool little guy—maybe a bit shy and kind of unpredictable but that was okay. It was becoming clear that being a single mom was no picnic, but Laney seemed to be doing a stellar job from my inexperienced viewpoint. Rocco was well-behaved and everybody seemed to love him.

Hell, I was beginning to think maybe my mom had the right idea about pairing my dad up with the kid. They'd been having their own little club meeting at the dinner table last night. Truth be told, I was a bit jealous. Huh, that was unexpected. I wanted Rocco to prefer me to my dad—maybe that was a bit juvenile but there it was. I made a mental note to look up some G-rated jokes on the internet.

But I'd gotten a yes from Laney for Wednesday and I was determined to win her over. Crap, now I had to impress her with my cooking, which I may have oversold a touch. Since spaghetti is just about the only thing I can cook, it looked like we'd be having Italian.

On Tuesday I got a call about another hiccup with a project out on the east side of town, so I spent most of the morning there. Bailey and I had met with Doug yesterday and, just as my mother predicted, he was eager to step up and help us out with some of this troubleshooting, paperwork, and scheduling. Today's debacle sealed the deal in my mind, and I was determined to call Doug in on this new issue and have him take it over. This new resolve had me grinning on my walk to my truck this afternoon. That's when my phone rang. *Laney.* My grin turned into a full-out smile and I believe I may have started to swagger.

"Hey, Beautiful, what's up?"

"Nate, thank God." She sounded harried.

"What's wrong?" I felt my stomach drop.

"Sorry, I didn't mean to panic but I'm in a bit of a bind and I didn't know who else to call."

My breathing returned to normal. "I'm glad you called me. What can I do?"

"I'm completely stuck here at work. We have a deadline that there is no way we can meet if we don't all stay late. Rocco's daycare closes at 6:15, Fiona is out of town, and Gavin's not answering his phone. It's already almost 5:00 and I have nobody to pick him up. Can you please, please, please pick him up for me and stay with him until I can get ahold of Gavin? Or can you somehow find Gavin and have him pick Rocco up? Anything!" She was sounding panicked again.

"Calm down. I got it. I'm done here so there's no reason to involve Gavin. I can swing by and pick up the squirt. Where's the school?"

She released a huge sigh. "Thank you, Nate. Thank you so much. I'll have to call the school and authorize you to pick him up first, but that won't take long. He usually expects me at about 5:15 so do you think you can go soon?"

I told her it was no problem and got the information I needed from her, including the spot where she hides the spare key to her house—on the top of the door jamb, if you can believe that. That particular hiding spot would be changing tonight.

Now that I knew she was feeling better and all was well, I thought a little bit of ribbing was in order. "I have to say I'm a bit surprised you called *me*, Laney. We're not even dating or anything."

"Shut your face, Sparky."

I drove up to Cornerstone Daycare around the same time as every other parent in town, it seemed. I showed my I.D. to the woman in the front office as Laney had instructed, and I found Rocco's classroom right where she said it would be. At least the teacher had told him to expect me instead of his mom or I'd be more apprehensive than I already was. It wasn't like the kid and I were super tight yet.

When I walked in the room there was a guy about my age directing his kid to get his belongings from the lockers across the room. "Tucker, grab your stuff—we've got to go!" The kid was wearing a bright pink shirt with the collar popped and dark blue shorts with—were those fucking flamingos? I looked back to the guy, expecting to find the mortified look any man whose kid was dressed like that should be wearing, but no, nothing. This guy's wife must either have his balls in a vice or be a champion at blowjobs.

I looked around for Rocco, confident that whatever he'd be wearing would be cool because, let's face it, his mom was awesome. I wasn't disappointed. Rocco sat at a table building a giant Lego skyscraper and wearing a t-shirt that said "Support Our Troops" and had a Stormtrooper on it. *Classic.* I also noticed he seemed to be humming to himself and his nose was doing that twitching thing again.

"Yo, Rocco!" I called so he'd know I was here. Before he could acknowledge me, the pink-shirted kid approached him.

The pussy-whipped dad motioned to the Lego table. "Is he yours?"

For some reason I didn't want to think about too much, I replied, "Yup."

The guy crossed his arms and nodded. "It's really great that he's in school with all the other kids … you know."

What. The. Fuck.

"No, I don't know. Please enlighten me." My voice grated and my body turned to stone.

He could not have looked more uncomfortable if a dozen Playboy bunnies had been pointing at his dick and laughing. "Just, you know, he's got some issues, right?"

And just then, out of the corner of my eye I saw the little flamingo bastard swing his hand and knock over Rocco's skyscraper.

We were done here. I used what I like to think of as my Bruce Banner pre-Hulk voice and laid into the prick with the perfect level of quiet power. "The only *issue* he has is that he's at a school with a bunch of stuck up assholes like you and your kid. Tell your kid if he ever messes with Rocco again I'll be giving my kid free reign to punch him in the nuts. And while you're at it, try growing a set of balls yourself and tell your wife to shop where they sell boy's clothes."

I stalked over to where Rocco sat dejectedly staring at his ruined masterpiece. "Hey, kid. Wanna get out of here and get some ice cream?"

His watery eyes came to mine and he twitched his nose. Then he nodded and took my hand.

One stop at SweetFrog (By the way, what ever happened to DQ?) and another at Home Depot and we were headed back to Laney's. Rocco remained pretty quiet, but I'd gotten a few smiles out of him and we'd exchanged a couple jokes. His were clearly made up and made zero sense but I laughed anyway. I'm no idiot.

I retrieved the "hidden" key, and after unlocking the door I placed the key inside the fake rock I'd purchased at Home Depot and set it in an inconspicuous place by the side door. I thought I would see if Rocco wanted to throw a ball around or play something outside, so I went in search of outdoor toys. The coat closet by the door seemed to be the best place to start looking; however, when I opened it an avalanche of purses, coats, shoes, and, oddly, unopened mail spilled around my feet. Hmm. What to do now? Since I didn't spot any sporting equipment, I decided to shove everything back in and pretend I'd never been there. It appeared Laney didn't mind a bit of clutter, to put it nicely. After that I thought it best to enlist Rocco's help, and we located a soccer ball in his bedroom.

I was no soccer player and it was safe to say Rocco was even less of one, but we still had a good time kicking the ball around the yard. We made up our own game, the rules of which he changed every time he started losing. I didn't care one bit. The kid and I were having fun. Rocco ran to the big tree in their backyard, declaring himself the victor, and I finally lay on the ground in submission. I stayed there for a minute looking up into the branches of the tree, and then Rocco came over and lay down right next to me. I put my hands behind my head and noticed him mimic my movements. It may have been the single most adorable thing I'd ever seen, and I felt a tug in my chest. Then a thought occurred to me.

"You know what you need, Rocco?"

"What?"

"A treehouse."

"For real?" His voice was filled with awe.

"For real. Let's build one."

His little fist punched the air. "Yes!"

And that's when I lost the first piece of my heart to that little kid.

When 6:30 rolled around we were both starving and nobody else was home yet. We'd gotten dirty playing soccer so Rocco's solution was to shed all his clothes. I opted to keep mine on, despite the aforementioned "pants optional" policy in place at Laney's house. I fixed us some peanut butter sandwiches and threw in a banana to make myself feel like a more responsible guardian.

Laney and Gavin both got home around 7:00. They walked in the door at the same time, and I heard Laney tearing into Gavin about keeping his phone charged. He threw an insult back at her and it reminded me so much of Bailey and me that I had to smile. Rocco and I were on the couch watching some asinine show about a bald kid with some weird-ass name I can't remember and his overly touchy-feely family. I don't even think Rocco liked it, but it was the only cartoon I could find.

"Hey, Nate," Gavin greeted us first. "Sorry about the daycare thing. I didn't realize my phone battery was dead."

"No problem. Hey, things are looking good at the new site. I hear you're picking things up pretty quickly."

Gavin scratched his head a little self-consciously. "Yeah, they're going pretty well. I'm learning a lot." He walked over to the couch and put his fist out for Rocco. "Hey, dude." They exchanged a fist-bump and he turned and headed for the hall. "I'm gonna hit the shower. I've noticed my luck with the ladies hasn't been so great when I head straight from work to the bars."

"It's a learning curve, my friend," I shot back.

"Hey, Rocco," Laney said quietly as she approached next. She was wearing a sheer blouse with some kind of black tank underneath and her ass was perfectly showcased, yet again, in a pair of tight black pants. It took everything I had not to pull her onto my lap and cop a feel. "I am so sorry I couldn't come get you today, buddy, but I promise I'll be there tomorrow." The guilt was plain on her face. Now I felt like a perv and instead wanted to pull her in for a hug. "Did you have fun with Nate?"

Rocco's head swiveled from the TV and his eyes were bright. "Mommy! Nate and I are gonna build a treehouse!"

Laney cocked her head at me, eyebrows to the sky. Perhaps this was the kind of thing you're supposed to discuss with the mom first.

Even though I may have been in trouble with Laney, my mood was sky high when Rocco gave me a hug on his way to bed. I waited on the couch and switched the TV to ESPN while Laney put him down. She emerged from his room fifteen minutes later and sat down beside me. I turned to give her my full attention.

She cleared her throat. "First of all, I want to thank you for picking up Rocco and taking care of him. I really don't know what I would have done if you hadn't come through for me." She placed her hand on my arm.

Before she could continue I said, "But I shouldn't have made plans to build a treehouse without conferring with you first. It didn't occur to me at the time, but I get it. I'm new at the whole kid thing so you're required to cut me some slack." I went with my most charming grin.

"Goddamned dimple," I heard her murmur.

"What was that?"

"Nothing. Yes, you're right. You should have asked me first but it's mostly just because I don't want you promising him things that don't end up happening for whatever reason. I can't handle him being disappointed any more than he already is."

I was sensing a much bigger issue at hand but I chose to let it go for now and try to tackle it later, once we'd gotten to know each other better. "You don't have to worry. I am 100% on board with the treehouse. In fact, I can't wait. I promise." I crossed my heart.

"I believe you. And thank you, Nate."

Well if that wasn't an invitation to go in for a kiss I don't know what was. But like a complete imbecile, I didn't. Instead, I chose that moment to fill her in on the little incident at daycare.

"Come here," I beckoned and made a space right in the crook of my arm. She didn't hesitate to fill it. Warm, supple woman cradled against me, I could be happy here for a long time.

"I take it things went well with Rocco," she said.

"They were actually awesome," I responded and I'm sure my excitement was reflected in my voice. "But I've got to tell you I was a little pissed about some things at his school."

Her body stiffened against mine. "What things?"

"Laney, I don't know if these people are your friends or if you just happened upon this daycare, but I did not get a friendly vibe, no offense."

"Crap." Her hand covered her eyes.

"It may have been a random one-off kind of thing, but some little prick was messing up Rocco's project and his dad was spouting off some bullshit about Rocco being somehow 'different' than the other kids. The whole thing just pissed me off and I told

the guy to go to hell and I may have even threatened his kid ..."
My voice trailed off as I realized for the first time how utterly
ridiculous this all sounded. Shit.

"You threatened a child?" Her jaw went slack and her eyes shot
fire at me.

"Well, maybe not so much the child but I'm pretty sure I
insulted the father's manhood and threw a threat or two in there."

Silence.

"In my defense, the kid was wearing women's clothing and still
had the nerve to knock over what I personally considered to be an
inspired Lego masterpiece that Rocco had worked hard on."

Laney looked down to her lap and then brought her eyes back
to mine. "Was the little fucker by any chance named Tucker?"

Feeling somewhat vindicated I responded, "Why yes, yes
he was."

"Okay, I can agree that I didn't get a good vibe from a lot of
the moms there, his included. But, Nate, you can't go threatening
people at daycare. Who knows how these things operate! They
could call the cops or something. Or at the very least we could be
kicked out for violent threats. You know they have these zero tolerance rules now?!"

"Well where are those zero tolerance rules when the pink-
shirted kid is bullying Rocco and his dad is insulting him along
with it? I don't know a lot about kids, but Rocco's skyscraper was
at least fourteen stories high and I believe an elevator was being
installed. Sounds to me like the simpletons couldn't compete so
they resorted to sabotage. Have you never seen a movie like this?
Rocco is the brilliant inventor and Tucker is the underachieving
mama's boy with something to prove."

She put one hand on my arm again and another behind my neck. "Nate, I need to hear the following words come out of your mouth: 'I understand these children are five and we are not in a Martin Scorsese movie.'"

I started to laugh but her facial expression remained deadly serious so I recited her ridiculous statement. Sheesh. But I added my own addendum. "Laney, I promise you there is nothing to worry about. Flamingo kid's dad was humiliated to the point where he will never utter a word of our conversation to another soul. Still, maybe shopping for a new daycare isn't the worst idea, huh?" Hoping I hadn't gone too far, I waited.

The next thing I knew I was being straddled by the hottest girl on the planet and I finally had her ass in both of my hands. Sweet Jesus, my life was good.

Chapter Fourteen

SCARLETT O'HARA HAD AN EXCELLENT POINT

*L*ANEY

His hands were on my ass and I was throwing caution to the wind. Every inch of my body was straining toward his, and each firm line of his chest, arms, and thighs was colliding with my body. My immediate thought was that we had too many clothes separating us, but we were in my damn living room so I had to stop my thoughts from careening that way.

His hard thighs were a dream and I wanted to strip his jeans off to caress them with my hands and mouth. Muscular thighs were a huge turn-on for me and Nate had them in spades. I don't know if it was just the physical labor from his job or if he did additional working out on the side, but his body was a thing of masculine beauty. I ground down on his pelvis from my straddled position and was not disappointed by the rigid evidence of his desire I encountered through the denim. It was obvious his body was as eager as mine, but I wasn't sure how far I wanted to go tonight. I was still freaked the hell out by him popping up in our lives only to disappear in a few months, so I knew I should be careful. I just had a hard time communicating that message to both my heart and my hoo-hah. He was so freaking hot. And he was so freaking into me. That was a collision of fates that didn't happen in my world. I was too weak to resist.

I ran my tongue around the shell of his ear and sucked his earlobe. Apparently that was the last straw. Nate physically picked me up and headed to my bedroom with his hands on my ass, and I had no choice but to hang on for dear life. This was shocking and a bit embarrassing on many levels, the least of which being the chronically untidy state of my bedroom.

Let me explain.

In all these romance novels, the buff guys are constantly picking the girls up and throwing them on the bed or having vertical make-out sessions—all while not straining a single muscle. I am not that girl. I have tits and I have ass, and I'm not saying that in some cute little "oh, look at her perky booty" kind of way. I have double Ds and a very proportionate ass to match. That very often puts me into the plus-size department and then on to a tailor to fit the smaller parts of me. Everyone loves to talk about boobs and booty like they are thrilled the old bombshell figure is back in style, but I can tell you two things: (1) a rack like this wreaks havoc on your back, and (2) tailors are not inexpensive.

So Nate carrying me to my bedroom, an event which should have been a romantic milestone complete with "Up Where We Belong" playing in the background, was instead an episode that filled me with self-doubt and imagined trips to the emergency room. A hernia, at the very least, was a distinct possibility in this little scenario—how romantic can you get?

Amazingly, though, we made it without injury and he deposited me gently on the bed. He honestly didn't look any worse for wear, and his lustful look implied I'd better kick my insecurities to the curb. Shit was about to get real. *Yowza!*

"You're wearing too many clothes," he growled while gazing at me from his elevated viewpoint at the side of the bed. "Lose the pants and the blouse. I'll take care of the rest."

Holy shit. It seemed someone was putting on his alpha pants.

His gritty voice and confidence were such a freaking turn-on that I couldn't comply fast enough. Clothes went flying and, lying there in my panties and black tank top, I looked up at him from my bed and couldn't quite believe this was happening. I couldn't even remember my last sexual encounter, which I'm sure I should have found depressing but, at the moment, my mind was very much otherwise occupied.

"You're so fucking spectacular." His pupils were large in his intense blue eyes.

Was this real? Nobody had ever looked at me like this before.

Still fully clothed, Nate leaned down and kissed my belly. He pushed the material of my tank up with his nose and began to run his tongue along my stomach, over my belly button and then across the top of my panties. "You smell so good," he murmured and then lifted my tank to reveal my black lace bra. He pulled the shirt over my head and then returned to hover over my breasts. "I can't believe how perfect you are," he said almost reverently. His eyes shifted up to mine and burned through me. "May I?" he asked, and

I felt so stunned and unsure, my hands just rested at my sides while he explored my body. I think they were as shocked as I was.

"Yes," was all I could manage.

His fingers grazed gently over my lace-covered nipples and they pebbled at his light touch. His lips then replaced his fingers and he began to lick and suck me through the lace. I couldn't stand it any longer and had to reach to my shoulders and pull the straps down so he could gain full access to my aching breasts. He groaned at the first sight of my dark rosy nipples before he covered them with his lips and tongue. I cried out when he lightly bit each one.

My hands, finally recovered from the shock of Nate's laser-focused attention, reached for him and I was beyond frustrated when I realized again that he was still dressed. Determined to remedy that, I clutched the hem of his t-shirt, skimming the dusting of hair on his lower belly in the process. I quickly stripped the shirt over his head and within a millisecond my hands were tracing every hill and valley of his shoulders, chest, and abs. Perfection. God, he was firm and smooth and his skin was incredibly sensitive if his occasional shivers were any indication. I could caress him all night and never get bored. Of course, I'd have to invite my lips and tongue to participate as well. I circled one of his nipples with my tongue and he responded with something between a groan and a laugh. God, I loved that.

Soon my playtime was over, it seemed, because his hands firmly gripped my wrists and held them to the bed while his mouth dove down to the waistband of my panties and took the lace between his teeth. He looked up into my face and I swear, at that instant, life as I knew it stood still. I don't know what it was but

something profound, something more than sex or teasing or friendship, gripped at my chest and I found it hard to breathe.

What did this mean? I'd never experienced another feeling like
it, and I could see in his eyes that Nate sensed it too. I felt heady
and strange and his look told me he was similarly afflicted.

"Mommy?" The door creaked open.

No no no no no! Rocco! I can't believe we didn't lock the door!

For some damn reason, kids don't understand that they are not
allowed to interrupt epiphanic moments. I threw a sheet over my
body and did my best to kick Nate onto the floor. (So sorry, Nate!)

"What's wrong, buddy? Why aren't you asleep?" My heart was
beating out of my chest.

"There are two reasons, but I can't 'member the first one."
Ugh. "I know the second one is that I need to bring a pack of new
crayons to school tomorrow," he said as he climbed onto my bed,
not noticing the shirtless man on the floor at the other side.

"That's already in your backpack, sweetie," I told him.

"I think the first reason is I need to sleep with you, but I don't
'member for sure."

Nate and I had been on the precipice of something profound—
but it was over for tonight. And while one part of me was
screaming to get it back right this second, the other decided to be
more rational. I was surprised I'd let things go so far in the first
place, except for the fact that I was insanely attracted to this man
and felt this intense pull toward him.

I maneuvered my way off the bed with the sheet still wrapped
around me, and tucked Rocco in with the remaining covers. I then
pretended to be a statue until his eyes closed and his breathing
slowed. Nate, who had also been impersonating a statue—one that

probably sported some bruises from his abrupt tumble to the floor —waited for my signal and then we both snuck out of the room. He pulled his shirt on as I walked him to the door. I wasn't used to having hormones coursing through my body like girls gone wild, so I was kind of twitchy during our goodbye.

He took my face in his hands. "I don't have to tell you that I'm really looking forward to our date tomorrow night. Is 6:30 still okay?"

I almost wanted to tell him to pick me up at 6:30 AM so we could finish what we'd started but I put my libido in check and agreed, "Sounds great."

He kissed me gently on the lips this time, and the contact was way too short. "Can't wait to see you tomorrow."

This was too perfect. I needed to come back down to earth. Any minute now, the wicked stepsisters would storm in and ruin my gown, and some super-hot girl (who did not have any baggage) would capture Nate's attention and steal him away. And then they'd both go riding off into the sunset back to Texas. That's how it works. What was I doing getting all excited?!

Still, I went to sleep with an internal happy dance and a big fat smile on my face.

Tonight was the night.

"Tonight is the night!" Fiona shouted. "Laney's gonna get laaaiiid, Laney's gonna get laaaiid!"

"Do you say anything anymore without the 'nanny-nanny-boo-boo' tone? I feel like we're eight years old."

"Well that would be extremely inappropriate given the subject matter."

This time I was at Fiona's where I could make use of her fashion arsenal. She was helping me with my hair and makeup, and then I'd dash home in time for Nate to pick me up. Gavin was getting Rocco from daycare and babysitting tonight so everything was organized. Except my nerves—they were in complete disarray.

"Am I moving too fast? Should I be doing this so soon?"

"Listen, the man defended your kid to a dickhead bully and then offered to build him a treehouse. I'd say you owe him at least a blowjob for that alone."

"Stop being so sentimental—you're gonna make me cry."

"Oh! Did I tell you Terrence is coming to town this weekend?" Fiona waggled her brows and did a booty shake—well, as much as she could with her non-existent booty. Terrence was Fiona's on-again-off-again "friend with benefits" or "fuck buddy" or "boy-toy" or whatever she was calling him these days.

He was a pilot and he was also a very fine specimen—tall, dark, handsome, with lean muscle. And while he didn't have a dimple, he did have this weirdly awesome slightly crooked smile that somehow always made you feel like you made him happy just by standing in front of him. In other words, he was a sweetheart, and besides the cool smile and all the rest, he had the most flawless deep brown skin I'd ever seen. There had been more than one occasion when I'd had a bit too much to drink and had oh-so-casu-ally run my hand down his arm just so I could feel it. Fiona caught me every time but she thought it was hilarious—she would, consid-ering after all the drinking was done, she got to go home to all that was Terrence. So it was a mystery to me why Fiona insisted on keeping things so light between them. I thought he was great for her.

"Fun ahead!" She continued the shake. "And I ordered the sweetest little silk Brazilian briefs from La Perla—they are the lightest pink with these lace panels—Oh! And I saw this ice blue bra and panty set that would look killer on you—please, please let me buy it for you!!" Her face fell at the shake of my head. "You're such a party-pooper."

There were certain things I would let Fiona and her endless money treat Rocco and me to, but La Perla? Not gonna happen.

"Hmm, I can't decide if he and I will go out or just order in and spend the whole weekend thinking up creative indoor activities. I hope the panties come before Terrence," she said.

Sometimes it was just too easy—I bit my lip to keep from laughing. "Well, it is still in the eighties most days so you'd really be saving yourself from the risk of sunstroke. It's the only responsible thing to do."

"I think you have an excellent point. So, what are we doing with this hair?" She led me to her vanity—yes, of course Fiona had a vanity.

"I don't want to look like I'm trying too hard so keep it simple if you can help yourself. And I'm wearing jeans so I don't want any arguments! It's just dinner at his apartment."

"Fine," Fiona pouted and ran a brush through my long hair. "But at least be civilized and borrow some of my jewelry, will you?"

We both regarded my reflection in the mirror as she twisted and pulled my hair, deciding on a style. A rock suddenly settled in my gut. My hands went to my cheeks.

Fiona dropped my hair and her hands held my shoulders. "What is it, Laney?"

"I don't know what I'm doing here. I just feel this, I don't know, *pull* toward Nate but I know he's going to break my heart. Rocco and I are going to get attached to him and then his dad will get better and he'll move away. You know I'm already worried about Rocco enough as it is, and here I am setting him up for another fall. What kind of mother am I?"

Fiona scowled. "You're the best kind of mother, that's the kind you are! You always put that little boy first and, sure, he's going through a little stress right now but you're doing the best you can. Where does it say you can't have a little something for yourself too? If Nate's leaving, what's wrong with a fling? And, anyway, you don't *know* he's leaving—you're making assumptions without all the information. You could just woman up and ask him outright, you know."

At the look on my face, she read that I was clearly not ready to "woman up."

"Just stop stressing. Hell, you could even find out tonight that you two don't really like each other as much as you thought. Then you're just out one treehouse, and you can get Gavin to learn how to form a right angle and put it together. The point is, just have fun tonight and worry about the rest later."

I considered her in the mirror. "Thanks, Fee. You're right. You have any wine?"

She looked offended. "Do I have any wine? Where do you think you are?"

I laughed at her and dropped my hands back to my lap. "All

right, pour some wine, pretty me up, and let's Scarlett O'Hara the shit out of this thing!"

I had a glass of wine while Fiona did her thing, and by the time the glass was empty my hair looked sleek and sexy and my makeup was a step up from what I'd normally wear but it looked awesome. I headed home to get dressed. Fiona did end up talking me into wearing a flirty skirt and some platform sandals from my own closet, and she made me text her a picture of my final outfit to keep me from cheating. Gavin and Brett were in the backyard tossing a baseball around with Rocco when the doorbell rang. At least I wouldn't have to deal with that awkwardness. I grabbed my purse, took a deep breath, and answered the door.

Nate was wearing a blue button-down shirt that drew attention to his eyes. The sleeves were rolled up to reveal his corded fore-arms and the first two buttons at his neck were left undone, affording me a glimpse of chest hair. His dark-wash jeans were a perfect fit, and gray Converse completed the picture. Comfortable, casual, and hot as hell. My lower belly warmed and the butterflies took flight. His jaw was freshly shaven for the first time and I wasn't sure which way I preferred it. His eyes were hot and they were focused directly on me.

"You look gorgeous," he said as his eyes roamed my figure.

"You don't look so bad yourself." *Was that my voice?* It was so breathy.

"Are you ready to go?" He crooked his arm out for me to take.

I wordlessly entwined my arm with his and we walked to his

truck where he opened my door and helped me in. Did he cop a bit of a feel in the process? Maybe, but I didn't mind one bit.

"So, what are the boys up to tonight?" Nate asked once he'd seated himself and pulled out onto the street.

"Lord knows. They were playing ball when I left so hopefully they'll stay out of trouble. Although Gavin's best friend is over so it's unlikely."

"You don't like him?"

"Oh, Brett's fine. It's just that when the two of them get together the chances for downright stupid behavior rise exponentially. I'm probably prejudiced, though, because Brett was there when Gavin got in a really bad accident one time and it ended up ruining his baseball career."

"I was wondering about that but I worried it was a sore spot so I didn't want to ask Gavin about it." Nate glanced at me. "After he met Gavin the other night, my dad mentioned that he used to watch him play when Gavin was in high school. He said everyone thought your brother would go pro one day but then never heard another thing after he went off to college."

"You were probably smart not to mention it—it's most definitely still a sore subject." I sighed.

"What happened, if you don't mind me asking?"

"No, it's fine." I smoothed my skirt and tried not to let the memories affect me. "He was playing on a full scholarship and was right on track to make it big. On his twentieth birthday he and Brett and some of their other friends had the bright idea to try out a teammate's motorcycle—having never ridden a motorcycle in his life, mind you." I shook my head at the thought. "Long story short, he broke his pitching arm in three places. Goodbye baseball scholarship. Goodbye big-league dreams. At least he'd had the good sense to wear a helmet. But, *then*, instead of recovering from the surgeries and finishing his degree, he chose to drink and become a bum. And I haven't quite been able to forgive him for it." I gazed out the window and Nate was silent. "Wow, that was probably more than you wanted to know." I forced a smile and looked back at him.

He glanced at me and then his eyes returned to the road. "Sounds very … complicated." That was a safe way of putting it.

I quickly moved us on to lighter subjects and we arrived at his apartment building minutes later. It was pretty dingy as a whole, with cracked sidewalks and weed-infested lawn spaces.

"I know," Nate said as he took my hand and walked me up the stairs to his second-floor apartment. "It's nothing to look at but it's cheap and it's only temporary. It was the only place I could find that would offer a month-to-month lease."

My stomach dropped. His comment removed any doubt I had about his plans. I had the sudden urge to turn around and run home, but the feel of his warm hand in mine somehow kept me anchored there.

He unlocked the door and it opened to reveal a small kitchen, an old sixties style table, and the ugliest couch I'd ever seen.

"Nate?"

"What?"

"Roseanne called. She wants her couch back."

"Who's the smartass now?" He elbowed me. "I borrowed it from my parents' basement. My real furniture is in Austin."

"I'm relieved I won't have to pretend to like your phenomenally bad taste." I smiled up at him.

He held a few strands of my hair and ran his fingers down until they caressed my collarbone. A shiver ran straight through me. "Let's reserve that thought until you taste my cooking. I hope you like spaghetti."

At that moment I thought I'd like anything he wanted to dish up.

Chapter Fifteen

BIG HEAD VS. LITTLE HEAD

𝒩ATE

"Well, that wasn't half bad if I do say so myself."
I leaned back in my chair and took a swig of my beer.

"I didn't realize there was any possible doubt. And it *was* good." Laney propped her elbow on the table and sipped from her wine glass.

Conversation over dinner had flowed easily. We talked about our experiences growing up in the same town and realized that we'd probably nearly met each other dozens of times throughout our youth. But with our age difference it wasn't so surprising that we hadn't. Then we moved on to her history with Rocco and his dad, a guy named Dominic who lived in California. The guy sounded like an assclown to me, but Laney was pretty laid back about it, so I obviously didn't have the whole story. It did explain, however, how she was able to afford a mortgage in a decent neighborhood while sending her kid to that stuffy daycare. I was guessing her job didn't pay enough to afford it all on her own. And I knew Gavin had only recently begun contributing.

Her relationship with her brother seemed especially complicated, as I'd noted earlier. There was obviously some tension there, but I liked the guy and by all accounts he was working his ass off and catching on really quickly at work. Regardless, the love between brother and sister was clear, and he was great with Rocco. Thinking of my relationship with Bailey and knowing the intricacies that exist between family members, though, I wasn't going to pry into that one. If Laney wanted to share, I'd let her do it in her own time.

She sat across from me, her hair all glossy and her eyes looking smoky and sexy as hell as her finger ran absentmindedly over the rim of her wine glass. My dick stood at attention—I'd been fighting a hard-on since the moment she answered her door in a short little skirt and sleeveless V-neck blouse that pointed the way to my biggest temptation. Damn, she was the definition of a bombshell and I couldn't wait to get her in my bed and under me.

"So, I'm guessing the home repairs are on hold in favor of treehouse construction?" she asked, taking another sip of her wine. I nodded and stood with my beer, motioning her to follow me to the hideous, but surprisingly comfortable, couch.

"Maybe so. The project has inspired me." I set my beer on the scratched-up coffee table.

That got a grin as she sat down next to me and I put an arm across the back of the couch behind her neck.

"I may have spoken too soon about the couch," she said. "This is actually more comfortable than mine."

"See, I do have good taste after all." I wrapped my arm around her shoulder and pulled her in closer. "About the treehouse, I've already drawn up some potential plans, but I won't know specifics until I take some measurements of the tree. It's going to be pretty amazing, though. Not to brag or anything." I grinned.

She beamed at me, then set her glass next to my beer and snuggled right into my side. If that's all it took to make her happy I'd build a hundred treehouses. I could see right down the front of her shirt and I didn't even pretend not to stare.

"I can tell you Rocco is beyond excited so that is music to my ears. It's really sweet of you to do this for him. It's sweet of you to do *all* the things you're doing for us. I feel like I don't deserve it." She put her hand on my thigh.

"Why would you say that? You deserve all sorts of good things." I turned her in my arms and leaned my head down to kiss her. She tasted of wine and her own unique flavor, which was quickly becoming a favorite of mine. The intensity of our clinch ratcheted up immediately as my tongue explored her mouth wildly, like I'd never get another chance. She moaned and arched her back, and we were soon leaning down into the couch, one of her hands fisting in my hair and the other squeezing my ass. I moved on top of her and ground my erection into the heated apex of her thighs which were still covered by her damn skirt. We were moving at lightning speed and it was hot as fuck.

"Nate," she breathed and began to pull away a bit, but she was trapped under me so I lifted up a few inches to give her some room.

"What's the matter?" We were both breathing heavily and my hand was caressing her thigh, moving closer and closer to the edge of her panties and the heat that waited there.

"I … I … I'm not sure." Her flushed face turned toward the back of the couch.

"Laney, look at me." She turned her face back and her hooded eyes met mine. "We don't have to do anything you don't want to do." My cock called me every name in the book, but judging by the look on her face, this was going no further tonight.

She put her hand to her forehead and I sat up, releasing her. She sat as well and straightened her skirt. "God, I feel like such an idiot. I really want this." She motioned back and forth between us. "I mean, I *really* want this." She attempted a smile.

I had no fucking clue what to do so I just shut up and hoped she'd clue me in.

"But I have more than just me to consider—I have Rocco. I can't just let someone jump into his life, play with him, build him a treehouse, and then just disappear. He won't understand that."

"Who's disappearing?"

"You know what I mean."

"Laney, there is no guarantee in any relationship. I don't know for sure what will happen between us down the road, but I can tell you that I am *more* than into you, if you can't tell that already." I raised a brow at her. "I can also tell you that while I'm seeing you I'm not even remotely interested in seeing anyone else—and I hope you feel the same way."

She nodded but still looked unsure.

I took a breath. "But I understand you're a mom and that has to come first. I just really want us to be able to spend time together and see where this goes." My hand reached out and she took it with hers.

"Can I have some time to think about it?"

My mouth said, "Of course." My dick said, "No fucking way!"

She gave me a small embarrassed smile and stood up, releasing my hand. "Thanks, Nate. I'm so sorry about … this." She waved awkwardly in the general direction of my lap.

"He understands," I said, and that got a laugh out of her. "Let me drive you home."

The ride back to her house was mostly silent and I did not have a good feeling about the way we were leaving things. I felt like I was missing some crucial piece of information, but I couldn't put my finger on it. I hated the uncertain feeling.

"Will you still come over to start the treehouse on Saturday?" she asked. "I know I'm sounding like a complete contradiction right now, but Rocco is so excited."

I shot her a smile. "Of course. I can't wait." We pulled into her driveway and I got out to open her door.

She stepped down. "Hopefully you guys can finish it before it's time for you to leave. Thanks, Nate. I'll call you." And then she kissed my cheek and ran to her front door.

I waited for the door to close behind her before I pulled out of her driveway. That bad feeling I had was turning worse.

By Friday morning I still hadn't heard one word from Laney and I felt a heavy weight in my gut. My only solace was that I'd at least get to see her tomorrow. I visited a couple sites already today to meet with some contractors, and I was pulling up to the Old Oak Ridge site wishing I could just drive down the street and knock on her door. But I'd promised to give her time and I knew she was at work anyway, so it made little difference.

As soon as I got out of my car I noticed Doug and Gavin walking my way.

"Nate!" Doug called. "I've got Gavin on framing but Mark mentioned he might pull him for some of that siding work. You know anything about that?" Both men approached and I adjusted the bag I was carrying.

I shook my head. "Don't worry about it. Stay on framing, Gavin."

"That's what I thought," Doug said distractedly and hurried away to address one of the contractors who'd just pulled up.

"How's it going, Nate?" Gavin asked, his hands perched stiffly on his hips.

"All right I guess," I responded. Gavin continued to stand that way and then I caught him clenching his jaw like he was mulling over a difficult problem. "Something wrong?"

"I don't know. You tell me." His voice was curt.

"Tell you what?" I was pretty sure I knew which direction we were headed.

"Dammit, I knew this would happen!" His voice rose and we got a few glances.

"What exactly happened, Gavin? I'm at a bit of a loss here."

He looked at me like I was stupid. "Laney. She's been in her room crying the past two nights, and it didn't escape my notice that the timing just so happened to coincide with the early end of your date the other night. So what the hell did you do to my sister?"

I was dumbfounded—it took me a few moments to speak. "Gavin, I didn't do shit. I thought things were going great and she's the one who put a stop to it. I've been the one waiting for her to call and tell me everything is okay."

"Well, shit!" He pulled his hard hat from his head and smacked it to his thigh. "Now I've got to wade into this like some fucking girl and find out what the hell is wrong."

"Don't worry about it—I'll get to the bottom of it. You can keep your man card. She's been hesitant about getting involved with me and it has something to do with Rocco and not wanting to have men going in and out of his life. But I swear I have no intention of ditching them, Gavin."

His hand pulled through his dusty hair and his shoulders dropped. "Damn, I think I get it now. It actually makes sense if you think about it. Rocco getting attached and then, when you leave for Texas, I guess that would suck for the little guy. It probably is for the best to just cut your losses." He dropped his hand to his side and put his hard hat back on with the other one. "Shit, I feel like I'm growing a vagina here. I gotta get back to work. No hard feelings, man."

He waved and left me standing there feeling like the most oblivious fucking moron on earth.

At 6:30 that evening I stood on Laney's front porch pounding on the door. "Laney, I know you're in there. I saw you peeking through the curtains!" I continued to pound on the door knowing that I was being a bit of an asshole but not caring one bit. My girl was in there and I needed to see her.

"Nate, please go away. I'm not ready to talk yet," she hissed through the door. "And stop pounding. I don't want to scare Rocco."

"Open the door and Rocco will be fine. Come on, Laney. Please."

I heard a frustrated huff, but the door opened a crack and I saw her beautiful face. I also saw the dark circles under her eyes and I cursed myself for the tenth time today.

"Laney, baby, please let me in. I need to talk to you—to explain."

Her will seemed to give out and she let the door fall open as she stepped back. I came through the doorway and wrapped her in my arms like I never wanted to let go. And in that moment, it was the God's honest truth.

"Where is Rocco?" I asked, careful not to say too much if he was close by.

"He's in his room watching cartoons on the iPad." Her voice was quiet.

I kissed the top of her head. "I think I get it now, Laney, and I am such an idiot," I declared.

She sniffled and spoke into my shirt. "That's usually a title I reserve for Gavin, but go on if you must." I loved that even when she was sad her sass came through.

"I don't know how I didn't see it before, but like I said, I'm an idiot. You think I'm moving back to Austin, don't you?"

She pulled back from my hold and looked up at me. "Well, yeah, eventually."

"Baby, I'm not going anywhere. I'm here in North Carolina to stay. It was always my plan to come back—my dad's heart attack just sped up the timing."

Her brows drew together. "But … but you kept saying all these things about 'temporary' stuff." I could see the wet in her eyes and I wanted to punch myself.

"I just meant that the apartment was temporary. I don't want to live in that shithole any longer than necessary." I smiled at her. "As soon as I have the time, I'm finding a house or a condo or something."

"Oh." That was all she said, eyes still teary.

"You forgive me for confusing you?" I leaned down and couldn't help but kiss her quickly on her sweet mouth. She just nodded, looking a bit dazed. I wanted to take her to her bedroom and show her how sorry I was, but I knew that couldn't happen for several reasons.

And despite my desire to pull her into my arms and assume that everything would work out perfectly, I knew I had to say one more thing. "But you know as well as I do that there are no guarantees in life. And I understand that you need to consider Rocco in all your decisions. I'm just asking for a chance, Laney."

Evidently over her shock, she finally smiled up at me and ran her fingers down my jaw. "By the way, if I have any say in it, I prefer the scruff." Then she reached up to me for a kiss. We wrapped ourselves around each other for several moments before cooler heads prevailed and we remembered the five-year-old down the hall, not to mention the open door behind me.

"Oh, I almost forgot." I turned around and retrieved my bag from the front porch where I'd left it. "Call Rocco out here. I've got some treehouse plans to go over with him."

Chapter Sixteen

GO ABOUT YOUR BUSINESS

*L*ANEY

I felt like I'd just won a free lifetime supply of dough-nuts, along with a magical guarantee that they'd never go to my ass, as I watched Nate and Rocco at my kitchen table poring over treehouse plans. I was also feeling a bit foolish for spending the last two days wallowing in misery when I should have just opened my mouth and asked Nate outright about his plans. Damn that Fiona for always being right. I resolved from here on out to voice my doubts and be clear about any reservations I had.

I also owed Fiona a call to let her know she could halt the cookie dough, wine, and ice cream brigade she was currently preparing. It was her weekend with Terrence, but since she's the best friend a girl could have, she had been checking in with me and was planning to stop by tonight before Terrence arrived.

"We're heading out back to take some measurements if that's okay," Nate said, stacking the papers and rising from his chair.

"Of course. But, Rocco, you're getting ready for bed in half an hour."

"Aw, man, can't I stay up later since Nate's here?" my kid asked, just like any other five-year-old would when presented with the opportunity to do something fun with a friend. No nose twitching, no shyness, no worried look in his big brown eyes. It seemed Nate was *in,* and I didn't care one bit that he was thirty-one instead of five.

"Just because we're building this treehouse doesn't mean I'm ignoring your house. I think tomorrow I'll go up on your roof to check things out. I'm also taking a look in your attic," Nate said as we were saying our goodbyes later in the evening.

"Are those euphemisms? I love it when you talk dirty," I said, trying to keep a straight face.

"They can be." He flashed a naughty grin. "But actually, I'm just giving you advance warning. I believe your attic access is in your bedroom closet and I wouldn't want to have to turn you over to one of those cable TV shows, if you know what I mean."

Shitballs! My secret wasn't so secret anymore. "Please don't tell me you've seen my closet."

"Okay, I won't tell you."

Double shitballs! My fingers started itching to do a little cheek rubbing. Nate grabbed both my hands before they could reach my face.

"I've decided to find your 'storage system' cute instead of scary."

"Oh God, you're probably one of those people who doesn't even have a junk drawer, aren't you?"

That was met with silence. Who was this guy? Oh, that's right, I forgot—he's Superman's brother. Superheroes don't have junk drawers.

"I have four junk drawers," I confessed.

He nodded slowly. "And, like I said, it's cute. I think. But I had to give you fair warning about the closet since I'll need to fit a ladder in there tomorrow."

He finally released my hands and I used one to smack him on the arm. "Haha. It's not that bad, you big jerk."

Nate's back rested against the wall by my front door. Rocco was safely tucked into bed—for the moment at least—but after the near miss with the little night stalker last time, neither Nate nor I were willing to enter the bedroom tonight. At this rate, we'd never get to do the dirty.

He pulled me in for an embrace. "I'm picking up lumber on the way over tomorrow so I'll be here about ten o'clock. And, Laney, we've got to figure out how to have a real date night one of these days." He growled and gave me a sweet kiss. I wanted to drag him back down the hall and have my naughty way with him, so I was already flipping through my mental rolodex to figure out how to organize some extended alone time for us.

"Definitely. I'll get to work on it." I smiled and kissed him back. My kiss may have been a little less sweet than his.

Well, it looked like I owed my vagina an apology. Before I could even ask Gavin to babysit I went and pissed him right the hell off, removing any possibility that he'd grant me a favor anytime soon. And the worst part was I thought I was doing something nice.

"Not interested," Gavin said over his shoulder as he tried to walk away.

"What do you mean? You're the perfect person for this, and it's just one night a week and one game on the weekends."

"I don't care, I'm not doing it! And stay the fuck out of my business, Laney!" He hitched his workout bag onto his shoulder and stormed out the door before I could stop him. *That went well.*

It was Saturday mid-morning and Charlotte had dropped by earlier to give me a plant she foolishly assumed I wouldn't kill. *Yeah* ... anyway, during the course of our conversation she mentioned that Aiden was signed up for rec league baseball and the coach had just dropped out. She asked if I knew of anyone who could fill in—her husband not being available since he traveled a lot for work. And, in her words, "He's about as athletic as a basset hound in a patch of sunshine." Sometimes I just loved the crap out of her Texas. So, naturally, I told her about Gavin. It was like kismet, or so I'd thought. Apparently, it was more like the worst misfortune to hit Greensboro, so fierce was Gavin's dismissal of the idea. Now he was pissed and I was evidently never having sex for the rest of my life.

Nate showed up at ten o'clock as promised. He and Rocco were out back doing lord knows what, but it seemed like each time I peeked out the window they both had their hands on their hips and were gazing up at the tree in deep thought. This project might take a while.

I still couldn't quite believe this guy was so interested in me—

truthfully, I didn't really feel like I had that much to offer. I knew if Fiona had been here she would have smacked me upside the head for talking trash about myself, but it was hard sometimes to keep a super confident attitude. I'd just have to go with it, though, because I wasn't about to give up a chance to be with somebody who made me feel the way Nate did.

I couldn't help but peek out the window again, and this time I was treated to the view of his cargo pants stretched tightly over his backside as he leaned down to lift a stack of wood. Damn that man could make me swoon.

Back to closet cleaning, Laney! Focus!

A few hours later Nate and Rocco retreated inside to escape the hot afternoon sun. I was fixing us some cool drinks while Rocco washed up in the bathroom when my front door slammed so hard the windows rattled. I thought maybe it was Gavin and he hadn't gotten over his hissy fit, but it was Fiona's petite form that came storming into the kitchen, stopping a few feet from me.

Her purse landed on the counter with a loud thwack, likely reducing its contents to dust. "I'm staying over tonight and I won't take no for an answer! I'm going to eat all your ice cream and watch tragically stupid teenagers on reality TV while you, my friend, are going over to your hot man's apartment and getting your muffin buttered." She pointed a threatening red-tipped finger at me. "I do not want to see your face until at least noon tomorrow and it had better look well-fucked. At least one of us should have an orgasm tonight and it sure as hell won't be me! Now tell Rocco his Aunt Fiona is inviting him to an ice cream party tonight and he can stay up as late as he wants."

When I didn't move she threw both hands out toward me.

"Shoo!" I still didn't move. This was "scary" Fiona—she didn't come out to play very often.

"Uh, Fiona, you remember Nate, don't you?" I motioned hesitantly to the pantry door where my "hot man" had been spraying WD-40 on the hinges but now stood stock still, the can suspended in his frozen hand.

Fiona didn't even flinch. "Hey there, hot stuff. You get all that?"

Nate just nodded slowly while the rest of him remained still.

"Can you please excuse us for a moment, Nate?" I asked as I dragged Fiona down the hall to my bedroom and closed the door.

"First of all, you can't come in here throwing out f-bombs while Rocco's at home and you know it. Second, I can't even believe you just said all of that in front of Nate. Just … oh God." I covered my eyes with my hand.

She huffed in dismissal.

I took a deep breath and shook it off. "And third, what happened? I thought you were doing sexy time with Terrence."

She scoffed. "Don't even talk to me about Terrence." And then she proceeded to talk about him anyway, as pretty much any girl would do. "What about 'friends with benefits' does he not understand? That man wants to, and I quote, 'take things to the next level.' What next level?! There is no next level! So I sent him to his hotel and told him that until he gets his head screwed on straight he needs to lose my number. I can't go back to my place in case he decides to show up to plead his case again." She did a full body shiver. *Dramatic much?*

"Wow," was really all I could say, though. Treading carefully here was essential. Fiona did not do commitment. She didn't do the girlfriend thing. She was kind of like a guy that way, but every other aspect of her was all girly-girl. I knew she had her reasons so I'd given up trying to convince her to give a guy a chance. But this was *Terrence*. They would be so good together. Ugh. I'd have to let it go for now, but hopefully she'd open the door a crack for him if he just gave her a little time. So, it looked like I'd have to give her a little time too. "I'm sorry, Fee." I gave her a hug and she finally let go of her mad a bit and sagged into my arms with a sigh.

"I know. Me too. Can I still eat your ice cream?"

"Every bit," I said, still holding her tight, my chin resting on the top of her head.

"You know, you really do have a great rack. It's like the best goose-down pillows in here." She tried to snuggle in.

I shoved her away. "You perv."

So it looked like the sex fates did like me a little bit after all. I'd gotten my sitter, although I would have preferred not to have involved Fiona's heart in the process. Nate, I could safely say, was even more thrilled than I was when I told him the news. And it seemed Fiona couldn't get us out the door fast enough. I barely had time to say goodbye to Rocco and elicit a promise from Fiona that more than just ice cream would be served for dinner.

"I need to stop by my place and take a shower, but then do you want to go out to dinner?" We were in Nate's truck and my nerves were jumping already.

"Sure, sounds good, but I'm not dressed for anything fancy." I motioned down to my casual black shorts and blue t-shirt.

"You look perfect to me."

"Aww." I couldn't help the smile I gave him.

The apartment building was just as neglected as I remembered and I didn't blame Nate for wanting to move somewhere nicer. Although maybe he should keep the couch after all, and just re-cover it.

He took my hand once again and led me to the door, not even letting me go to unlock it. Once the door closed behind us, I found myself pinned to the wall beside it and Nate's mouth was on mine. He tasted like the lemonade I'd fixed him earlier, but his mouth was warm and his tongue hot as it pushed past my lips to explore mine. My hands immediately found his thick hair and gripped the back of his neck. I melted into the kiss. Then my hands decided to do a little wandering as his lips left mine and traced a path down my jaw to my neck. On their journey, my hands found their way beneath his t-shirt and began exploring the planes of his abs and back. He smelled faintly of sweat and some kind of spicy shampoo or aftershave, and I was turned the hell on.

"Sorry," he murmured into my neck as his hands rounded my ass. "I'd really intended to take you out and make this romantic but that's gonna have to wait till next time. I need you to get naked right now." Well okay, I guess this was really happening. Holy crap!

Patience was obviously not one of his virtues because he had my shirt pulled over my head in a heartbeat and his hands moved quickly to the button on my shorts. I was feeling both overheated and a bit self-conscious at the same time. Why was it so bright in here? Would he like what he saw once I lost all my clothes? Wait, why was I the only one getting naked? *Again!*

"Quid pro quo." My voice was breathy as I stilled his hands and motioned for him to lose his shirt. I also may have helped a little, letting my hands take their time on the upward journey over his stomach and chest. Lord, was he built. "How do you look like this?" I blurted out.

He laughed. "Look like what?"

"All muscle-ey and bumpy and stuff." *Brilliant, Laney. You should write a book.*

He laughed again. "Well, I run every morning, and construction work isn't exactly sedentary. I also hit the gym a couple times a week." He shrugged. *He shrugged.* If I exerted that much energy I would be dead within a week.

His hands grazed over my taught nipples still encased in my sensible white bra—I really needed to take Fiona up on her offer to sex up my lingerie. "Now, can we get back to the fun stuff?" Nate asked, dropping his hands down to my shorts again.

"Yes, please."

After that we couldn't get undressed fast enough, and although the couch was comfy and all, that was definitely not where the deed would be done if I had anything to say about it. As our clothes were coming off I subtly aimed him toward the bedroom. We fell onto the bed, me in just my panties and him in black boxer briefs, the rest of our clothes littering a trail from the front door. I had to take a moment to lift myself up a bit and admire the view. He was even more breathtaking than I'd imagined—the perfect proportion of leanness and muscle. I took in his wide shoulders, sculpted chest and abs, muscled thighs, and just the right amount of hair covering his chest and leading a trail down to the hardness that waited under his boxer briefs. It seemed while I was conducting my perusal he was doing some investigating of his own and, if the heat in his eyes was anything to go by, he liked what he saw. That gave me just the boost of confidence I needed to go up on my knees and shimmy my panties down from my hips. I didn't get far, though, before he flipped me onto my back and settled himself between my thighs, only the thin material of his briefs separating our heat.

"I'm gonna spend a while here if you don't mind," he said before tracing one of my nipples with his tongue. "Go about your business and I'll let you know when I'm done."

I tried to laugh but it came out as a gasp instead as his teeth nipped at my peak. He let out a little growl and continued to worship first one breast and then the other. My hands roamed his shoulders and hair, and my breath was coming out in pants after a few minutes—I needed him to do something, anything, just *more*. "Nate," I pleaded.

His tongue began a path from my aching breasts to other aching parts farther south. "I know it's only been a few weeks, but I've been dreaming of this for what feels like forever." He groaned as he parted my lower lips and swiped his tongue upward, ending at my clit and sucking it into his mouth.

I may or may not have had a stroke at that moment. I was no longer in control of my faculties as I started making sounds no human should ever make. Nate Murphy was one seriously talented man. Once his fingers joined his tongue, I was arching and keening and holding his head in place as if the fate of the world depended on him continuing to give me head like it was his fucking job. After what seemed like only seconds, I came in a rush of ecstasy and delirium, and I'm pretty sure Fiona could hear my cries from my house and was raising an ice cream spoon in tribute.

Nate lifted his head and looked only slightly less satisfied than I imagine I did.

"Oh my … I mean … oh my … that was … oh my." Yep, I was a poet.

He smiled at my orgasm induced dopey-ness and wiped his mouth on the sheet. "I'll be right back—gotta get a condom." And he walked his fine ass to the attached bathroom.

I did some internal cheering and dancing (in which I was very graceful) and rolled over onto my stomach to wait for his return. I whipped my head around when I felt a sharp pain on my left butt-cheek.

"Ow! Did you just bite my ass?"

He looked way too smug. "Yes I did. And I plan to do it again."

"Oh my God, what is wrong with you?" I laughed and rubbed my sore ass.

"You've obviously never seen your ass."

I rolled my eyes at him. "Speaking of, you'd better lose those shorts or I'm ripping them off *your* ass."

"Oooh, aggressive. I like it," he teased.

And then I lost patience and kind of lunged for his junk. I'm not really clear on how it went exactly, but the important part was he got naked.

Chapter Seventeen

LIFE IS GOOD HERE IN THE BATCAVE

*N*ATE

I think Laney may have actually torn my boxer briefs as she yanked them off me. I had evidently awakened some inner vixen in her. Not that I was complaining. Or thinking. At all. She had my cock in her hand and was stroking me with perfect pressure and rhythm from base to tip, circling the head before moving back down. It was so good, I was worried things would be over before they began.

"Baby, let up a bit. That feels way too good." I stood at the side of the bed while she lay on her stomach, her ass arched up in the air and her hands all over me. I couldn't get enough of the view. Or her taste. I could have gone down on her for hours with her silky thighs cradling my head, but I was way too anxious to get inside her. She was all soft skin and lush curves.

I pulled her hands from me. "Turn over and scoot up the bed." I tore the condom wrapper with my teeth and tossed it over my shoulder. I then rolled the condom on and settled between her thighs, covering her lips with mine. I knew her taste was still on my lips and the idea that she could taste herself made me that much harder. "Is this okay?" I wanted to make sure since the last time we'd been here she had backed off.

"Yes," she whispered, and I began to press slowly into her wetness. "Nate," she murmured, her eyes closing. "You won't hurt me. You don't need to be careful."

That was all I needed to hear before instinct took over and I thrust all the way inside her. She was hot, wet, and fucking tight. I groaned as I pulled almost all the way out and thrust back in. Her returning groan told me she was feeling the same ecstasy I was. She started moaning and meeting my thrusts, and then her legs wrapped around my waist and I was done for. I thrust away like my life depended on it, our skin slapping together and our sweat mingling on our bodies. I brought my mouth back to hers in a frantic kiss.

She cried out her release against my mouth and I followed her a moment later. I couldn't comprehend this experience—it was like no other I'd ever had. I wanted to hold her and fuck her and keep her in my bed for an eternity. In essence, I was screwed.

"So, is Laney short for something or is that your real name?" I asked her a little while later. We were lounging on my bed, wrapped up in the sheets.

"Oh God," she replied. "I'll tell you but only if you promise not to ever use it."

I crossed my heart.

She flopped onto her back, her head resting on my pillow and her nipples almost revealed by the shifting sheet. "It's short for Elaine. I think my parents were obsessed with Seinfeld. There were even some hints dropped that I may have been conceived during an episode, but my brain refuses to go there. Anyway, it's just always been 'Laney' and I am more than fine with that."

"I think 'Elaine' is pretty."

She rose back up onto an elbow and gave me a skeptical look.

"But you're definitely a 'Laney,'" I reassured, not being a complete rookie.

That seemed to satisfy her. "What about you? I know your full name and I've met your family, but tell me more."

"Well, let's see. You know I've always been into building things—and you know I can't wait to get back to it, of course. Oh, speaking of which, did I tell you my dad started visiting the office for a few hours this week?"

"No. That's great!"

"Yeah, my mom is not too keen on the idea, but she knows he needs to get out a bit or he'll suffocate. Oh, and she wanted me to tell you he's been fiddling around with the fishing gear you brought by. And he may ask to take Rocco fishing sometime soon."

Laney looked like I'd just presented her with a litter of newborn kittens. "Oh my God—that is so sweet. I'll have to run it by him first—he can be shy and a little hard to read, but they seemed to get along great at your parents' house so I bet he'll be excited. We may have to go along, though, just to warn you."

"I wouldn't mind that at all. I'll get you into a swimsuit and we can go off on our own and stir up a little trouble."

That got me a shove.

"You hungry? We never had dinner." I had to feed my woman.

"Starved. Do you have some clothes I can throw on? I'm not sure where mine ended up."

I got out of bed and put my boxer briefs back on—looked like they weren't ripped after all. "I prefer you naked, but I guess I can find something for you." I rummaged in a drawer and pulled out a t-shirt and a pair of athletic shorts.

"You're a prince among men, Nate."

"What are you in the mood for? Chinese? Pizza? Thai?" I asked as I walked toward the kitchen. I got no response. "Laney?"

"Oh, hell no!" was all I heard from the bedroom. I went back to investigate and found her wearing my t-shirt and throwing the shorts on the bed like they'd done something to offend her.

"What?"

"How is it fair that your shorts are too tight on my ass? I could hardly pull them up!"

Having been a guy for thirty-one years, I knew there was no right answer to that question. Silence, however, did not seem to be one of my options. "I love your ass. It's perfect." She still looked unsettled. "If you recall, I actually tried to take a bite out of it I loved it so much."

She still pouted and it was fucking cute. "Whatever … let's order Chinese."

Phew. I might actually be good at this relationship stuff.

We ate delivery Chinese in bed, managing not to make a huge mess, and we talked about everything and nothing. I told her more about my dad and how we were all struggling with the changes that had to be made. We also talked about Austin and my life back there—a life I wasn't missing at all anymore. She told me more about Rocco's dad and about Gavin and some of the struggles her family had been having. After dinner and some more conversation, I finally ended up taking that shower, but it was considerably more fun with Laney. Maneuvering in the tiny stall was a challenge, but we managed. And the next morning I felt quite proud when we walked into Laney's kitchen and, upon examining Laney's face, Fiona gave us a golf clap.

One Month Later

This last month was perfect. Well, actually, that's a lie. One thing I learned is having a five-year-old underfoot is a recipe for constant blue balls. But outside of that, life was amazing. Laney and I spent every possible moment together, and I didn't know about her, but I'd never felt this way about another girl. I was trying not to think about it too hard and just enjoy. We had to get creative about the locations and times we had sex due to the afore-mentioned little cock-blocker, but let's just say her shower got a lot of action—and, luckily, it was considerably larger than mine. I still hadn't spent the night, though we'd discussed it. She was going to sit Rocco down for a talk this week and feel him out a bit. I knew she trusted me, so I was glad I wouldn't have to jump that hurdle again.

As for work, Doug and my dad had all but taken over the administrative headaches (although my mom constantly looked over Dad's shoulder and tried to keep him on a short leash). I was back to getting my hands dirty. If I'd had to conduct one more bid-development or client meeting, my head would have exploded.

I took over as foreman on the Old Oak Ridge project and helped out at a couple other sites during the downtime. I still couldn't answer the neighbors' concerns about potential tenants, but Laney trusted my good intentions, and her word seemed to be good enough for everyone else.

Halloween was just around the corner and we were sitting on Laney's back patio enjoying a perfect fall afternoon. A cool breeze blew in and the sun was starting its descent, coloring the sky that perfect shade of orange. Rocco squealed out in the yard as Fiona chased him up the ladder of his completely amazing and innovative treehouse—if I do say so myself.

"That thing is ridiculous." Laney shook her head and laughed at me, knowing that I was admiring my own work. I just winked at her. I knew she loved that treehouse almost as much as Rocco did. It had a ladder with safety handles (Laney's idea) and a split-level design with built-in seating and a table. It also had porthole windows and even a pulley system to haul up important kid stuff. If I had a treehouse like that when I'd been his age I would have charged a cover to everybody who came over to play.

As it was, only Rocco and all of us adults had been inside so far, which I knew still bothered Laney. But I thought Rocco seemed like a perfectly happy kid. He was hardly even doing the nose twitching thing anymore, and he was anything but shy with me.

And the best part? Laney pulled him from that "up their own asses" daycare and he was now in a much smaller program run out of a former teacher's house. Charlotte's son went to the same place when she worked at her part-time job, and by happenstance a full-time spot had opened up in the daycare. Laney snatched it up and Rocco was much more at ease with a smaller and less asshole-ish group—my term, not Rocco's.

We had all gone over to Charlotte's house last week and I'd seen the two boys playing together. I'd also seen the gleam in Laney's eyes and could feel her relief. Next step was an invite for Aiden to play in the treehouse, which I liked to refer to as "The Batcave" but Rocco had dubbed "The Fart Fortress." You can't win 'em all. Oh, and in case you're keeping track, I did indeed apologize to Charlotte for being an asshole the first time we met.

"You know what you need?" I asked Laney as I glanced around the yard.

"Uh oh, what now? You've damn near fixed everything in my house and you already have a list a mile long of upgrades you want to make."

I pretended I hadn't heard her. "You need a screened-in porch. I bet you'd spend a lot more time out here in the summer if it weren't for the damn mosquitoes."

She turned to me, flashing some leg in her cut-offs and making me want to haul her to the bedroom. "Nate, I would love a screened-in porch, but you have got to stop doing all these things for me. You have enough to do with work and you haven't even started to look for your own place."

Yeah, about that. It was no mistake I hadn't started looking for my own place. I knew it sounded crazy, but I was in love with this girl and I was jumping ahead in my mind. It seemed ridiculous to buy a place when she clearly loved this house and I was seeing a future with her and Rocco. And besides, The Batcave was here so there was that. But I knew she wasn't ready to go there yet, so I kept quiet except for a small "Meh." It was the most noncommittal noise I could come up with.

"Meh? You're weird."

"And you're pretty." I leaned in for a kiss.

"I think I'm gonna be sick," Gavin's voice came from the back doorway.

I removed my lips from his sister. I could see things from his perspective—if I had to watch some guy pawing Bailey I would probably feel a little ill myself. Gavin wandered out onto the patio and took a seat next to me.

"I'm going to grab a drink. Anyone need a beer?" Laney asked, rising from her chair.

"Sure," Gavin and I responded simultaneously as Laney went into the kitchen.

"Is it strange that I'm jealous of a five-year-old?" Gavin asked, taking in the treehouse and the two faces peering out the window.

"If we're talking about Fiona, I can't answer that, dude. If we're talking about the treehouse, I'm right there with you."

"Definitely the treehouse. I can get laid without pissing my sister off, thank you very much."

I laughed at the mental image of Gavin hitting on Fiona with Laney as a witness. "Smart man."

Gavin sat forward in his chair and put his elbows to his knees. "Hey, I know it's late notice, but do you think there's any chance I can take Thursday off? There's somewhere I've really got to be and I can only do it on Thursday."

"Shit, man," I started, not looking forward to what I had to say next. "You haven't earned any vacation days yet, and if I let you take off it sets a bad precedent. It puts me in an awkward position, especially considering Laney and all, but I have to say no. I'm really sorry." I shook my head. I hated having to do this, especially to Laney's brother, but the rules are the rules and if I let one person break them then it's just a slippery slope. That's not the kind of work environment I can tolerate.

He looked like he'd already known the answer before I told him, but I still felt bad.

"Hey, no problem. Just thought I'd ask."

An awkward silence settled until Laney came back out with the beers and a glass of wine for herself. She hollered out to the tree-house, "Hey, any of you adventurers thirsty?!"

"Only if it starts with 'w' and ends with 'ine'!" Fiona shouted as she and Rocco descended the ladder.

"Who do you think you're talking to?!" Laney answered and headed back into the kitchen.

Fiona and Rocco approached the table, Fiona rubbing at her hands trying to wipe the dirt off. "I swear this red clay dirt is so hard to wash off sometimes."

"You should use douche," suggested Rocco as casually as can be, wiping his own hands on his jeans.

We all froze. Well, all of us but Rocco. His only parent was out of earshot, and the three of us were waiting for each other to come up with the correct response. Nothing.

Just as Laney emerged from the house, Gavin hissed at Fiona and me, "Do. Not. Tell. Laney. I like my balls where they are."

Chapter Eighteen

NOW ACCEPTING APPLICATIONS FOR A CORNER MAN

*L*ANEY

It was official. I was in love. And everything all those damn movies and romance novels said was true. Well, almost. Nate couldn't get it up ten times in a night, and doing it against a wall was ridiculously difficult, not to mention entirely impractical. But all the parts about food tasting better and jokes being funnier and finding yourself with a great big smile during a boring-ass meeting? All true. It was a little like being drunk but still able to operate a moving vehicle and hold down your day job. I was saying hello to complete strangers at the grocery store and complimenting them on their outfits. I was singing in my car and getting caught by other drivers at stoplights and not caring in the least. All I had to do was think about that sexy man and I turned into a fool.

Neither of us had said the words yet, but I had a hunch his heart was right in line with mine. Or at least I hoped it was. Not a day had gone by without Nate sporting the scruff I told him I liked so much, so that had to mean something, right?

And everything else was going well too. Rocco liked his new daycare a lot better, and he was even starting to engage with some of the other kids. The nose twitching was still around sometimes but was not nearly as prevalent as it had been. And he and Nate were getting along phenomenally. Now I just had to tackle asking Rocco how he'd feel about Nate having "sleepovers" at our house. Part of me felt like it was too soon, but my gut was telling me this was *it*. Nate was *the one*.

I'd finally introduced my parents to Nate over Skype last week. Yeah, that wasn't awkward at all. But since we'd spent a few evenings with his parents already, he said it was time to meet mine. Luckily Rocco dominated the online conversation as he usually did, so it all turned out okay in the end.

Fiona was still in a Terrence-free zone but hadn't had a date with anyone else as far as I knew. She and Nate got along well too, which was a big bonus since she and I were a package deal. And Nate being Gavin's boss hadn't turned out to be as troublesome as I'd feared. They hung out like friends when Nate was at our house, and Gavin still appeared to like his job, so all was good.

Until it wasn't.

It was Thursday after work and Nate let himself in the front door as usual. Rocco and I had been home for a little while and I was chopping vegetables, pretending to know what to do with them, while Rocco watched cartoons in the living room. As soon as Nate entered the kitchen I could feel a weird vibe. He didn't come over and kiss me right away like he usually did so that was my confirmation that something was wrong. He dragged his fingers through his sweaty, matted hair and set down his hoodie.

"Hey, mind if I jump in the shower? I'm a mess."

"Sure. You okay?"

"I don't know …" he hedged. "We'll talk later."

That did not sound good. Not at all. My first instinct was to follow him into the bedroom and make him talk. But I forced myself to think like a guy and I left him alone for the time being, as he'd asked.

Dinner was very quiet. Gavin hadn't come home to eat, which wasn't unusual, but it would have been nice to have someone else to relieve the tension at the table. Nate was stewing, and even Rocco's chatter wasn't enough to rouse him. I just spent the time responding to Rocco and asking him about his day.

When dinner was over, Nate grabbed his hoodie and started to open his mouth to speak. I cut him off before he could get one word out. "You don't need to tell me everything if you don't want to, but you don't get to leave here without saying at least something." I leaned against the stove and waited.

He set his sweatshirt back down and then his hand went back to his dark hair. "It's nothing, it's just … well, have you seen Gavin today?"

I looked at him warily. "No. I usually leave before he gets up. Did something happen to him?"

"No, I don't think so."

I pushed off from the stove. "Stop worrying me, Nate. Wasn't Gavin at work today?"

"No. He never showed."

"Are you sure? Maybe he was at a different site today or something."

"Laney, I'm his foreman."

"Well there has to be a good reason, right?" But I was feeling uneasy all the same.

"I'm pretty sure there's a reason all right." He sighed and then threw his hand out to the side. "This sucks."

"What aren't you telling me?" My hand was predictably glued to my cheek by this point.

"Gavin asked me earlier this week if he could take today off. I told him he hadn't earned vacation yet so the answer was no."

"Okay, that makes sense. Why did he need the day off?"

Nate's hand was back in his hair. "He didn't say. He just said he had something he needed to do and it could only be done today. But he seemed okay when I turned him down."

I approached him and laid my hands on his chest. "Nate, I'm sorry he put you in this situation. I hope there's a good explanation and this can all be worked out, but it sucks that you were put in the middle like this."

"No, it goes with the job, regardless of who my girlfriend is." His hands ran up and down my arms. "The problem is now I'll have to dock his pay and put him on probation. I'm worried he's not going to take it well and I don't want him taking it out on you. He can be pissed at me, but he knew the consequences, and I know things can sometimes be tense between you two."

He wasn't wrong. And I was pissed and disappointed that Gavin had put Nate in this position. Things had been going so well, and I thought the big dope had finally grown up a bit. Where in the world could he be and how could it be important enough to risk his job? Not to mention disrespecting Nate like that.

"Listen, I'm sorry I'm being so moody. If it's okay with you I'm just going to go home. I don't really want to run into Gavin tonight and I'll have a more level head in the morning if and when he shows up to work."

I told him I understood and gave him the biggest hug I could muster.

Damn you, Gavin!

It was eleven o'clock when I heard the front door shut—smoothly, thanks to Nate's handy-work. Gavin's footsteps were hardly audible and I'm sure he assumed I was asleep, not waiting on the couch to strike like a freaking rattlesnake—which was exactly how I felt.

"Where in the hell have you been?"

He jumped, his palm hitting his chest. Good, I scared the shit out of him. He quickly regained his composure. "None of your business, *Mom*. Go to bed."

"It is my business when, (a) you have me worried you're dead in a ditch somewhere, and (b) my boyfriend is your boss and you decided to play hooky like you're sixteen again and put him in a really difficult spot." I didn't even try to hide my annoyance.

He stalked into the living room and dropped his bag on the floor. "See, I knew it was a bad idea for you guys to date. I totally saw this coming!"

"You saw yourself acting like an irresponsible dipshit again?"

His mouth went tight. "I wasn't being irresponsible. I weighed my options and decided the consequences of skipping work were worth it."

"Oh, this should be good. What exactly could have been more important? Were you donating a kidney?" My brows shot up and I leaned back into the cushions.

"Don't be such a bitch. I went to see Coach Willis." He inched closer to the couch.

"Why?" I was utterly confused.

"He called me up this weekend and told me he'd be in Charlotte and wanted to see me. But he was only going to be there today. I thought … I thought. *Goddammit!* I thought he was calling because he wanted me back on a team. I don't know what the hell I was thinking, I just got the call and I couldn't *not* go." He slumped onto the couch next to me, his head dropping back.

Well, shit. The guy looked like a kicked puppy, so I calmed myself down a bit. "What did he really want?"

Gavin choked out a humorless laugh. "He's got some camps he's working with and asked if I wanted a temp job coaching some kids. And he said he missed seeing my ugly mug, so he wanted me to come in person."

I didn't know what to say.

"I don't want to coach some snot-nosed kids. I want to *play*. I was supposed to play."

I remained silent and rubbed his arm. My heart broke for him.

But only for a second because then he went and pissed me right the hell off.

"I'm quitting the construction job and going to Virginia."

At his words, my back went so straight I could have taught an etiquette class. "You what?! Are you joking?"

"No. I'm just not cut out for this."

I could almost hear the countdown to my brain's imminent explosion. "Not cut out for what? Being an adult?" The calm I'd regained was a thing of history. I leapt off the couch and pointed right in his face. I couldn't have stopped myself if I'd tried—the urge to rant at him had been bottled up for so long.

"You lived in Mom and Dad's house for two years and never got a job—never paid a dime. You let them buy you a Jeep, for Christ's sake—it may be a shitty one but you still let them pay for it. They were so afraid you were going to fall apart and so disappointed *for* you that they would have done anything—and you let them!

"You acted like a spoiled child whose favorite toy had been taken away and you let them wait on you hand and foot. It only took eight weeks to recover from your injury—an injury that was a direct result of your own goddamned carelessness, by the way—but you milked the hell out of it and acted like a whiny baby. You took advantage of them and refused to grow the fuck up and take responsibility."

My blood was on fire and I couldn't seem to stop. "So life didn't turn out how you wanted it to—join the fucking club. Do you think I lay in my bed as a child dreaming of my future life as a single mom pinching pennies and working a boring-ass job to make ends meet?" I swiped my hair out of my face and kept going. "And don't you even think about throwing the help I got from Mom and Dad in my face. I know I was damn lucky to have them and I appreciated the hell out of it. Never did I take it for granted, and I pulled my weight as best I could. I got dealt a bad hand and took it on the chin, unlike you. I picked myself up and moved on because that's what it is to be an adult."

I was so worked up by this point I felt like I needed a corner man to wipe my face down.

But Gavin, who had been swiping my finger aside repeatedly, was up and facing off with me. He had come to fight too. "You got dealt a bad hand?! Ha! You decided to spread your legs for some douchebag with a guitar and suffered the consequences. I chose to get on that motorcycle and you chose to be a slut, so don't paint me with a different brush, Laney. We both fucked up. The only difference is that my fuck-up killed the only dream I've ever had in my entire life! Yours just changed the timing of what your life had in store for you anyway."

He laughed without a trace of humor. "You got an awesome kid out of your fuck-up, and if I asked you on your worst day if you'd change one thing about how your cards fell you would always say no because a yes would mean you wouldn't have Rocco. You ask me the same thing and I'd answer yes every single time. I would give anything to change that night and get my career back. There is no fallback or plan B. There's nothing." He stepped into me and his voice dropped.

"So you go ahead and be all superior and call me an idiot like I know you love to do, but you will never understand what it's like to be me and lose the one dream you ever had. You've got Rocco, you've got your new house, you've got your perfect boyfriend, and you've even got the fuckwad California kid to fund your life. Wow, I feel so sorry for you!" He sneered and backed away, grabbing his bag again.

Then he turned and headed for the door. "Now, if it's all right with you I think I'll go get drunk with Brett. Because, unlike my sister who's supposed to have my back, he has never failed me. Tell Rocco I'll catch him tomorrow and tell Nate whatever the hell you want to."

I hurried to catch up and stepped right in his way. "You don't get to drop the mic and stomp out of here." I poked him in the chest. "You talk about your dead dreams and, yeah, it sucks ass that you didn't get to play pro ball, but you could do *anything* else in the world! You didn't even bother to finish college. Mom and Dad were standing there, money in hand, offering to help you finish. You could have picked *anything*, but getting drunk with Brett was what you chose—it's what you always choose!"

He tried to push me aside but I wasn't done. "And as for my dreams? I never even had a chance to figure out what they were—I didn't get the time to. I was going to get a four-year degree and a chance to figure out my future on my own time. Instead I'm stuck in a cubicle for the rest of my life doing a job Brett could probably do hungover."

Gavin rounded on me and shoved his finger in my face. "You're so full of shit. You curse me for taking advantage of Mom and Dad and then you tell me I should have taken their money for college? Which is it? And if you hate your job so damn much, why don't you just quit?!" he hissed in my face and pushed me aside to reach the door.

"God, you're such a child! You don't get it at all!" I yelled at him.

He flipped me off, proving my point, and slammed the door behind him, making me feel so agitated that I wanted to scream and throw things. Why couldn't he see that he had the world at his feet if he'd just open his eyes and consider the possibilities waiting out there for him? *Son of a bitch!*

I checked on Rocco to make sure we hadn't woken him up, but thankfully he was fast asleep, upside down on his bed. I felt utterly crappy and there was no way I'd be able to sleep, so I called Fiona, praying that she was still up. I got her voicemail. Well, reality TV it was, then.

Nate: *Did Gavin ever show up last night?*

Laney: *Yeah, and we got into it. I'm pretty sure we've disowned each other.*

Nate: *I've done that to Bailey numerous times but she's still somehow hanging around.*

Laney: *I don't think he's coming to work today. I'll explain everything later, but I'm really sorry he's being such an ass.*

Nate: *Can't wait to hear this one. Have a good day and I'll call you later.*

Laney: *XOXO*

Nate: *You know I can't bring myself to do that crap.*

Laney: *Oh, come on, just one lousy emoji or acronym and I'll leave you alone ...*

Nothing. Damn.

I had just arrived at work and really should have been doing my job, but I had to catch up with Nate—and I still hadn't heard from Fiona. I'd been so pissed off the night before that I'd tossed and turned and waited for Gavin to come home, but he never showed. Not a huge surprise. So, I was basically a zombie this morning, my Diet Coke doing nothing to revive me. I barely made it through the day, and I may have possibly nodded off on the toilet in the early afternoon. If the pins and needles in my butt-cheeks were any indication, I probably did. Is it bad form as an employee to bring a pillow into the bathroom?

I texted Fiona again and finally got a response. "ttyl sorry," was all it said.

By the time I picked up Rocco and got home, I just wanted to pass out. Thank God it was the weekend. I followed Rocco in the door and was pleasantly surprised to find Nate standing in my kitchen making dinner. "Oh my God, I love you."

Yes, that's what I said. *Shit fuck damn!*

Being the wonderful man he is, after a silent beat he just turned around and smiled, flashing me the dimple.

"Can we please just pretend I didn't say that and you come here and give me a kiss instead?" I pleaded.

That got a good laugh and the kiss wasn't so bad either.

"Hey, dude," Nate addressed Rocco after making my belly dip. "I'm making homemade pizza. You want to help?"

"Yeah, yeah, yeah!" he shouted.

"Go wash your hands first," I told my kid, "and keep your clothes on—naked people are not allowed to prepare dinner. It's a health code violation!" He raced to the bathroom, probably ignoring what I said.

"Well," my arms circled Nate's waist and I rested my head on his firm chest. "You seem to be in a much better mood tonight."

"Yeah," he said. "Sorry about last night, but it's all worked out … well, for the most part. We'll talk about it once Rocco's in bed."

This was a revelation to me because I hadn't seen nor heard from my pain-in-the-ass brother since he stormed out of here last night. I was dying of curiosity. But instead of pressing Nate for details, I joined in the pizza-making party and contributed to the total mess my kitchen became. It was pretty awesome.

I put Rocco in the tub after dinner and hoped the flour and sauce that coated his entire body would all wash off. Tonight's song was about pooping in The Fart Fortress so I tried to stay out of the bathroom as much as possible. I have a dirty mind, don't get me wrong, but Rocco's is a totally different variety of dirty I can't quite connect with.

To my shock and great pleasure, Rocco requested that Nate read him his story before bed. This had never happened before, and I could tell Nate was pretty touched, though he macho-manned his way past it like it was no big deal. Afterward, I gave Rocco a kiss and tucked him in, pleading with him to stay in his own bed.

"But I like yours."

"I know, but you need to learn to stay in your own bed all night."

"Why?"

Because I can't sleep very well with your butt in my face.

Because I want to get laid by my boyfriend and you're kind of cramping my style.

Because I love you but mommies need personal space.

But no, I went with, "Because I said so." I had finally done it— I'd turned into my mother. Good God.

Unbelievably, he actually accepted my answer, but I was pretty sure it was just because he was so tired. I would never get that lucky again.

"So, tell me how this whole Gavin thing worked itself out. I didn't sleep a wink last night I was so worked up. I'm glad it got sorted."

Nate and I were on the couch, me with my glass of wine and a pillow snuggled in my lap, him leaning back with his legs resting on the coffee table and an IPA in hand.

"Well, I have to say I was pretty pissed last night and I wasn't sure what to expect this morning. He didn't show up—"

"What?!"

"Let me finish. He didn't show up at first. Then around ten o'clock he came and found me. He looked like shit. Then he laid it all out for me like I assume he did to you last night, and we worked out a deal. His pay for yesterday is being docked and he's on probation, but I'm letting him make up the couple hours he missed this morning."

"So he's not quitting," I stated more than asked.

Nate looked uncomfortable.

"Now here's the part you may not like. He's not quitting … for now." I started to react but he put a hand up to stop me. "Listen, Laney, I don't want somebody working for me who doesn't want the job. That's how mistakes get made and people get careless. That can only result in shoddy work and injuries, neither of which I need. If he doesn't want to work construction then he shouldn't."

"But he doesn't want to do *anything*!" My anger from last night was resurfacing.

"You know that's not true. He wants to play baseball."

I almost choked. "But he can't! A gazillion doctors and trainers have told him that. It's over—no big leagues. He needs to get over it and grow up." I set my wine on the coffee table so I wouldn't spill it—or throw it.

Nate put a hand on my leg. "Look, I don't know if he can or can't play, but if he wants to try, that's *his* business, not mine, and frankly, it's not really yours either."

"Excuse me?!" My blood pressure hit the ceiling and I threw the pillow down, knocking Nate's hand aside in the process.

"I know you've been dealing with this situation for a lot longer than I've been in the picture, but I saw the look in his eyes when he was talking about playing. It's his passion—his dream. I know what it's like to be forced to do something other than what you love and it sucks."

I couldn't stay seated any longer. "I can't believe I'm hearing this. Since when am I the only person on earth who is in touch with reality?"

"Cut the sarcasm, Laney. Usually I think it's cute but right now is not the time." Nate sat forward and set his beer down too.

"I'm sorry, I just don't know how else to respond when I'm faced with not one but two delusional people who think you can just wish on a star and all your dreams come true—poof! That's not how life works, and encouraging Gavin will just lead to heartbreak in the end."

"Who's heart? If he wants to risk it, let him."

"Everyone's heart, Nate! Everyone's! That's what happens when people you love make bad decisions and you're left standing as the only responsible person in the room, no matter how much you wish you could say, 'Fuck it! I think I'll skip work and go to Paris tomorrow—that sounds like a shitload of fun!'"

Nate stood and put his hands out in a "let's placate the crazy person so she doesn't shoot" manner. "Okay, I can see I've touched a big nerve and you're getting emotional. Let's take a step back—"

"Emotional? Emotional?! Oh, so now I'm just the hormonal female fucking things up by bringing feelings into it. Oh, and I probably have PMS too so obviously my opinions are invalid!"

"That's not what I said and you know it!" He was starting to get pissed. I should accuse *him* of having PMS.

This was getting way out of hand. "I can't talk to you right now. I think you should leave."

"Come on, Laney. This is crazy!"

Tears pricked my eyes. "Of course it's crazy—the entire world seems to have turned inside out and I'm the only one making any sense!" I physically turned him around and started pushing him to the door. "Please just go. I can't handle any more of this right now."

"I don't want to leave things like this, Laney," he protested but let me lead him, even though he certainly possessed the strength to stay put.

I started to cry. I couldn't help it. "I can't … I just … I need you to leave me alone for now."

I think the tears did him in because he finally caved. "I'll go home but we're going to talk tomorrow and work this out."

I continued to push him out. All I could do was shake my head. My mind was so discombobulated and the tears wouldn't stop. I felt my heart breaking but I wasn't entirely sure of the source.

"I am so sorry! I had to go to Raleigh for one of the charities—my mother guilted me into it—and everything was so last minute. Gary was pissed so I'm probably fired, but that's actually a good thing. He was starting to flirt with me and you know I don't go there. I've got something else lined up anyway, I think. So I ended up spending the night because my dad got off work and we all went out to dinner. One wine led to another and I stayed at the hotel where the function was. So, what did I miss?" Fiona chattered over the phone.

I laughed but it held no humor at all.

"Oh no! What happened?"

"I have no idea. I mean, I do, but I don't. I think my brother is moving to Virginia and I think Nate and I may have broken up." The tears started again for the tenth time since last night. I'd had to call Charlotte for emergency babysitting this morning because I didn't want Rocco to see me upset—so at least I was by myself while I cried my eyes out. Two nights without sleep and with too many tears—I was shriveling up like a raisin.

"What? No! That can't be true," Fiona protested.

I proceeded to tell her everything I knew, ending with me shoving Nate out the door.

"You really told him you loved him?"

"That's all you took from that whole saga?" I sniffled

"Of course not, but I wanted to focus on the good stuff."

"There is no good stuff. And to top it all off, if I broke up with Nate and Gavin is leaving, I'm essentially stripping my poor kid of his two best friends. Just hand me my 'Mother of the Year' award right now," I sobbed.

"Oh stop. All of this can be fixed. Just listen to your fairy godmother, Fiona, and it will all be okay."

She proceeded to calm me down a bit and try to put things in perspective a little better. My exhausted mind wasn't working very well, but some of what she said started to make a little sense.

"You and Nate did not break up. What you did was have a fight —all couples have fights—and once you patch things up you get to have hot make-up sex. I've known you for years and when you get going there is no stopping you—you're sort of like a *Housewife* in that sense—I hate to be the one to break it to you."

"Hey—that's mean. You're supposed to be making me feel better."

"Oh shut up—you know it's true. Now, listen. I love you and I only want the best for you and Rocco. You've not had the easiest time of it, but I need to lay it out for you, Laney, so please don't be mad at me."

"Oh God—what? Is this the part where you tell me I'm not always 100% right?"

"Yes it is, girl, and you can handle it so here goes." She took a deep breath and dug in. "I think the reason you get so worked up over Gavin and his admittedly sketchy life choices is that you may be projecting a little bit. You're not happy with some of the choices you've made, and after you beat yourself up a bit, you tend to turn it around on him. Maybe you're reluctant to treat him with more patience and compassion because you can't stop being mad at yourself for your mistakes and decisions that didn't work out too well."

I could picture her perfectly on the other end of the phone. She undoubtedly had her bottom lip between her teeth and her eyes were squeezed shut. I couldn't speak as I tried to process what she said and not throw the phone down.

Silence. My wheels turned for another minute.

"Fiona?"

"Yeah?" Her voice was barely audible.

"Did you just fucking Dr. Phil me, you little whore?!"

"Maybe." Her voice went up an octave.

"Aw hell. I'm gonna have to grow some lady balls and dish out some apologies, aren't I?"

"That would be my recommendation, yes." Her normal tone returned. "But I don't think you're wrong about Gavin needing to man up. I think you just need to adjust your sensitivity level a touch. And maybe we should both stop calling him an idiot so much. I think maybe 'bonehead' sounds more supportive. No—I've got it—we can call him a 'boob.' It gets the message across but will give him happy thoughts!"

"Have I told you lately how much I love you? Or how weird you are?" I was actually smiling at this point—a minor miracle given the last couple days.

"No, but it's a given. So, if you're feeling a little better, I have some phone calls to make and a couple errands to run."

"What are you planning, Fiona?" My back prickled with apprehension.

"Never you mind. Like I said, let your fairy godmother take care of it." And then she hung up on me.

Chapter Nineteen

HANGOVERS AND SOFT UNDERBELLIES

*N*ATE

"You should always listen to me, man. Getting serious with a chick? Not worth it." Mark took a deep swallow of his beer before setting it back on the table. When he'd seen what a pathetic mess I was this afternoon, he convinced me that a night out drinking and playing pool at Jake's was just what I needed. I was pretty sure I was wasted because Mark was beginning to make a lot of sense.

"Yeah, you're probably right. I bet I could get a girl here to go home with me and she wouldn't get all emotional and bat-shit crazy." I looked around the bar half-heartedly for a suitable woman. Ah, shit. What did it matter? None of them was the one I wanted.

"Dude, I hope for your sake you didn't tell Laney she was bat-shit crazy."

"No way. I'm not that stupid." I took another swig of my beer. "I may have called her emotional though."

Mark threw his head back with a maniacal laugh. "That's even worse. I can't believe how ignorant you are. That's like rule number one on the list of things never to say to a woman you want to nail."

"You're such a romantic, Mark. I can't believe you don't have a girlfriend."

"Believe it, man. That's the last thing I need. Keep it light, keep it fun, and keep it comin'—that's my motto." He toasted me and I toasted him right back, though my heart wasn't really in it.

"Well, would you look at this." A familiar voice joined in. I turned my head and, after it stopped spinning, I saw Gavin and his friend Brett by our table, beers in hand. "I didn't think I'd see you here tonight. I figured you'd be hanging with Laney and the little man. I'm still a bit scared to go home so I've been hanging at Brett's."

I gave Gavin the fakest smile I could muster. "I want to kill you."

"What did I do?"

"I think Laney broke up with me. I may have defended you and in the process broken some unspoken rule about siding with siblings in an argument. It's all quite … fuzzy."

"Shit. Are you serious?" He cocked his head.

"It's either that or she's insane," I offered.

"Ah, I'd go with insane."

"Unfortunately, it doesn't matter if she's crazy or not because I'm in love with her." My filter-less, alcohol-addled brain prompted my mouth to speak.

"Dude," said Brett.

"Fuck," said Gavin.

"Christ on a bike—seriously?" said Mark.

"Yup," was my response to them all.

Everyone was quiet, contemplating the fucked-up nature of my situation. We all took a swig of our beers.

"All right." Gavin moved first. "Let's fix this." He took hold of my arm and tried to pull me from my barstool. The world tilted a little. Hmm, that was odd. "Shit, you're wasted, aren't you?"

"It seems that way."

"Okay, I'm driving you home and we'll go to Laney's in the morning and iron all this out. You got a couch I can crash on?" He supported me and led me toward the door.

"Yup, and according to your sister, what it lacks in style it makes up for in comfort, if I'm remembering that correctly."

"Don't do that. It's too pathetic. The less you speak from here on out, the better."

I awoke to shit in my mouth.

Okay, well not literally, but I imagine that's what shit tastes like. I looked around and realized I was lying in my bed but had absolutely no recollection of how I'd gotten there. There was also a small hammer inside my head beating away at my brain to the tune of "You Asshole. Why Did You Drink So Much?" I hadn't heard that one in quite some time. I chanced sitting up and it only got a little worse. I could do this. A glass of water and three ibuprofen rested on the upturned packing box that acted as my bedside table. Thank God, somebody liked me.

Carrying the glass, I shuffled carefully into the living room and found Gavin sitting on my couch fiddling with his phone. Oh yeah, now I was starting to remember.

"Yo," was all I could manage. I swallowed the pills and winced.

"Hey. You're alive. It was touch and go for a while there last night."

"Yeah, sorry about that. I don't usually drink that much."

"No problem." He shook his head. "If I could count the number of times I ... well, maybe not the most appropriate story for my boss. But, considering the current situation ..." He laughed.

Yeah, I felt like a moron. "Right. So, am I missing any important details from last night?"

"Oh, wow, this is awkward. You mean you don't remember proposing to that stripper last night?"

My stomach dropped right to the floor and I thought I was going to be sick. What the fuck had happened last night?

"Joking, dude. But you should see the look on your face." He was enjoying himself way too much. I would have to remember to punch him in the face when I was feeling better. "Seriously, though, I feel bad that I was the cause of this mess. Laney and I? We just ... I don't know. We're kind of like oil and water sometimes and you just got caught up in it. Don't worry, though, I've got a plan."

One diner breakfast—or more accurately, lunch—of grease topped with grease and a side of grease, and I was feeling much better. I still didn't know if I trusted Gavin to fix my Laney problems, but it couldn't hurt to let him try.

After we ate, Gavin drove us to Laney's house. I was extremely leery—she'd asked me to leave her alone and I really didn't want to get slapped in the face or punched in the nuts. "I don't know about this, Gavin."

He put the car in park and turned off the engine. "Do you trust me?"

"Not even a little."

"Hm. I guess I can see that. Let's put that aside for the moment. Can you answer one question for me?"

I nodded.

"Is it possible for me to work for you part time instead of full time?"

That was not where I thought he was going with this. "Yeah, sure. We've got several part-time guys. It would affect your benefits, but yeah."

"Good. Now let's get in there and get your girl." He paused getting out his door. "And if you tell anyone I said that I'll kick your ass."

"Afraid to show your soft underbelly, Gavin?" I had to rib him. I got out and we started up the front path.

"Fuck you," he grunted.

Before we could get to the porch, the door opened and there was my girl—or at least I hoped she was still my girl. Her hair was pulled up into some kind of messy thing on top of her head and she was dressed in a loose t-shirt and cut-off shorts. Her face was free o makeup and I spotted dark circles under her eyes. She was perfect. Her eyes came straight to me.

"I've been trying to call you. I was worried you never wanted to see me again." Her eyes filled with tears.

"What?" I pulled my phone out of my pocket. Dead. "Shit. My battery's dead. I'm sorry."

"No, I'm sorry—so sorry, Nate, I—"

"All right, let's not give the neighbors a show—get your asses inside," Gavin directed. Laney didn't even spare him a dirty look. Huh. We proceeded indoors and Gavin shut the door behind us.

Laney faced me with her hands to her cheeks. "I was mad at Gavin and I totally took it out on you and I shouldn't have. I said some awful things and I didn't mean any of them. Well, some of them I did but those were more about Gavin, not you."

I stepped closer and pulled her hands down so I could hold them. "I'm sorry too. I shouldn't have stuck my nose into a situation I didn't fully understand. And I probably said some things I shouldn't have either. Can we be done fighting now?"

"Yes, please." She threw her around my neck. I squeezed the living hell out of her in return and kissed her temple.

"Okay, okay, let's stop while we're still at a PG rating. I have a few things I need to say," interrupted Gavin.

Laney and I pulled apart and she turned to face him. I moved behind her and wrapped my arms around her waist.

"I have some things I want to say to you too," confessed Laney.

Gavin tipped his chin. "I'll let you go first if you promise it won't involve yelling. Or punching me in the junk."

She crossed her heart. "I couldn't even if I wanted to—Rocco's just down the hall. Look, I know we fight and that's kind of our thing, but I owe you an apology. I haven't been very sympathetic these last couple years and it probably has more to do with my own issues and insecurities than yours, or so my fairy godmother told me. And—"

"Your fairy what?" I had to interject.

"Never mind—that's not important. Anyway, Gavin, you're important to me and I love you. And I really appreciate all the help you give with Rocco. I'll try to be more supportive and less judgmental from here on out. I promise, and I'm sorry." She released a breath like it had been weighing her down like a ton of bricks.

"Wow." Gavin blinked. "That was … kind of unexpected." He laughed self-consciously and scratched his head. "Um, I was gonna tell you I'm sorry too."

He backed up against the wall and tucked his hands in his pockets. "After our fight on Thursday, I went over to Brett's to get drunk and I started ranting to him about my pain-in-the-ass sister." He shot Laney a sheepish look. "But he kind of hit me in the face with the same truth-stick you did. Nobody besides you has ever gotten on my case about getting my act together, and to hear it coming from him was kind of a kick in the nuts.

"You're my sister and you're supposed to nag me and be full of shit, but he's been my best friend through all this and he said he couldn't keep his mouth shut anymore. So, I've been thinking a lot about it the last couple days and I'm finally coming to terms with the fact I won't play ball for a living. But that doesn't mean I can't play at all—which I know you've been trying to tell me, so just shut up, okay?"

Laney relaxed back into me as Gavin continued, "Anyway, I

made a few calls and then I received a few more. It seems your fairy godmother has some connections, because I have an interview for a job at the Baseball Academy coaching high-level teenage players. It wouldn't be full time, but Nate said I can still work part time with him, so I think I'm gonna go for it. Hell, what is it they say—those who can't do, teach?"

"Something like that," she responded.

Gavin raised a hand to rub over his chin. "And, Laney, I know you worry and you're afraid of making mistakes, but you're not a screw-up—and I shouldn't have called you a slut either."

My ears perked at that one. It was one thing to get into a fight but another entirely to call my girlfriend a slut. Laney must have felt my body tense because she moved one hand to my thigh to keep me in place.

"The same night you and Dominic were getting your drunken deed on, there were hundreds of other couples on campus doing the same thing. The only difference was yours resulted in a pooping, crying, booger-laden, eighteen-year-long commitment while everybody else got to sleep off their hangovers and move on with life."

We all smiled a bit at that one, and Gavin continued, "If you asked anyone what kind of mom you are to that kid, there isn't anybody who wouldn't sing your praises. You didn't screw up his life and you're not going to. You're the love of his life and that is pretty fucking awesome. So, that's it. That's all I've got." He threw his hands to the sides.

"Get your ass over here and give me a hug, you big boob," Laney said in a tight voice, and I let her go to her brother.

"Boob?" he asked.

"Yeah, I'm trying it out." She enveloped him in a bear hug.

Gavin smiled over her shoulder. "I like it."

Gavin took Rocco to the park to give us some alone time and we made the most of it, combining a much-needed shower for me with some unbelievably hot make-up sex. Laney came at me like a sex-crazed wildcat and I had the marks on my back to prove it. It made the last miserable day almost worth it. We lay in bed afterward, her cheek resting on my chest and her arm thrown over my waist.

"You know, I've been doing all this thinking about Gavin and his ruined dreams. One of the things that's always bugged me was that I didn't *have* a dream that could or couldn't be fulfilled. I guess I felt like you get what life gives you and you move on, but that's not really the best attitude, is it?" My fingers traced lazy circles on her back and I let her talk. "I guess I could learn a thing or two from you and Gavin. If there's something I feel passionate about, I shouldn't let anything stop me without trying my hardest to get it."

"And what do you feel passionate about?" I kissed the top of her head.

She reached down and copped a feel of my ass. "Besides your hot ass, you mean? I don't know—maybe owning an alpaca farm?"

"Seriously?" My fingers stopped their movement.

She laughed. "No, but it sounds interesting, doesn't it? I don't like to shovel shit, though, so that's probably out."

"Probably. What else?"

"I don't know. But I do know I'm only twenty-five and I've got time to figure it out."

"I forgot I was dating jailbait." I pretended to push her away.

"Whatever, old man." She smacked my chest.

"So, there's something I've been thinking about too," I said.

"What's that?" She snuggled back in my crook again.

"You."

"What about me?" I could feel her smile against the skin of my chest.

"Well, there's that awful temper of yours. And then there's your hoarding habit—don't get me started on what I unearthed in your hall closet the other day. And then we have the issue of your cooking—I have to say it's only slightly better than my mother's, and I'm worthless in the kitchen too, so we're kind of screwed. Oh, and of course there's your habit of rubbing your cheeks like you're trying to summon a genie—"

"Is this going somewhere?" she asked, raising her head to look at me with narrowed eyes.

I nodded and smiled. "Yup. What I'm trying to say is I love you."

Her cheeks pinked at my words. "You've got a strange way of expressing yourself, big guy."

I shrugged. "I figured it's easier to list the things that are so very wrong about you than to list the ones that are so very right—I can't really count that high."

"Well, if that wasn't the most romantic thing ever—you big jerk." She smacked my chest again and started coming in for a kiss.

"I guess I forgot to add your violent streak to the list. I'll make a note."

"You do that." And her lips met mine.

EPILOGUE

*L*ANEY
One Month Later

"This was such a great idea, Laney. We should make this a tradition." Erin linked her arm in mine as we stood enjoying the sunny afternoon on the back porch—oh, excuse me, back *deck*.

Nate and I had compromised and I agreed to let him build me a deck instead of the screened-in porch he wanted. I told him he could always finish it off eventually, but for right now I was sticking to my guns. He'd spent so much time and money fixing up my house that I had to draw the line somewhere. Of course, he couldn't make it just any old wood plank deck—he had to add built-in seating and a nook for his kick-ass grill he'd finally brought from Austin.

It was the day after Thanksgiving and I, like any sane person, was avoiding all retail locations. We were hosting an open house of sorts and invited practically everyone we knew to drop by throughout the afternoon to hang out and snack on leftovers—which we supplemented with burgers and brats. Maybe Nate couldn't cook all that well, but the man could *grill*. He explained that grilling was a skill that came along with having a penis—and something else about cavemen cooking meat over a fire, a topic which his dad had been strangely enthusiastic about discussing. Not that Erin would allow Riordan to have any of the grilled meats.

After a token protest, Riordan summoned Rocco to the deck. "Come on, Rocco. I'm going to show you how to clean a fish. Then maybe I'll be allowed to use the grill." With the unseasonably warm weather, they'd gone fishing on Thanksgiving morning and had a bit of luck. So fish had been added to the menu for the day.

I looked over at Erin and said, "Actually, it was Nate's idea, but I agree. It feels like more of a holiday when you can spread it out over a couple days. But I'm kind of shocked I got Fiona to come over. I figured she'd be in retail heaven."

"I heard that." Fiona approached. "I was up at five o'clock this morning, thank you very much, and I may have even bought a few things for you, my friend—of the sexy variety, if you know what I mean." She winked.

"Uh, yeah, I think we all know what you mean. And thank you for talking about this in front of my boyfriend's mother."

"I was young once too, so don't worry about me. And besides," Erin said, squeezing my arm, "Rocco could really use a sibling, don't you think?"

Danger! Danger! Need immediate rescue from the crazy lady!

As if reading my thoughts, Nate walked up and stole me away

from his mother. "Leave her alone, Mom. Go bug Bailey about having babies. I think I saw her flirting with someone inside."

"Really?" Erin's eyes lit up and she couldn't get inside fast enough.

"Thank you." I hugged Nate back. "Who is Bailey flirting with, just out of curiosity?"

"Nobody. She's stuffing her face with pie." He grinned.

I laughed and looked around the yard where our friends and family mingled. My parents were here, having come back to town to celebrate the holiday with us. Rocco was over the moon. They were staying at a hotel, an arrangement that would never be repeated if Erin had anything to say about it. Our families had spent Thanksgiving together and were getting along great. Thankfully both sides had a high tolerance for crazy.

Some of the guys and gals from Nate's work were here too, and I recognized a few of them, specifically Mark with the cock-sure smile and Doug who, for some reason, was wearing a Hawaiian print shirt for the holiday. I also noticed that Mark hadn't taken his eyes off Fiona since she walked outside. *Oh my*.

Nate made his way back to the grill and announced that the food was ready. People wandered over to fix a plate. It didn't escape my notice that Rocco wasn't among them. I spied his little head through the treehouse window, along with that of Aiden and one other little girl from their daycare. If that view wasn't a balm to my soul, I didn't know what would be.

"Hey, Shortcake." A male voice sounded behind me. I turned around to see Mark lean back on the deck railing next to Fiona, doing the oh-so-casual arms crossed to show off my big biceps thing—*hey, it's a thing, trust me*. He was also giving her that super cocky smile and I almost felt sorry for him. He had no under-standing that the phrase "big things come in small packages" was coined with Fiona specifically in mind.

"You talking to me, Meat-head?"

Oooh. This was going to be fun.

Gavin came over, draped his arm around my shoulders, and whispered in my ear, "Excellent. Dinner *and* a show." I snorted.

"Hey, I was just trying to say hi. You don't need to be insult-ing," Mark said to Fiona.

"I was just returning the favor. Run along now." She shooed him away.

Ouch.

Mark's eyebrows rose. "I was also gonna tell you that the kids' table is inside, Tinkerbell."

Not bad.

Fiona's jaw tightened. "What a coincidence because I was just going to tell *you* to go eat a bag of dicks."

Hmm, an odd choice, but it hit its mark anyway.

"Are you always such a bitch to people you just met?" His casual stance was long gone and they were in a face-off.

"Only to complete morons." Fiona's mouth curled in distaste.

"What is your problem? Jesus, I don't need this crap." Mark stalked into the yard and away from my charming little bestie.

Fiona, completely unfazed, stepped up to the grill and grabbed a plate. "Oooh, are those sausages? I love sausage. Give me a big one, Nate."

Gavin and I both started snickering, and Nate shot us a death glare.

After we'd all eaten and most of the crowd dispersed, I sat on Nate's lap—he insisted and I'd learned not to question him on his opinions about my body. I sighed the sigh of a completely contented Laney.

"I love this day."

He kissed my temple.

"Oh, hey," Nate said suddenly. "I forgot to tell you. We rented the last space in the Old Oak Ridge property." The project was wrapping up and they'd already signed rental agreements with a financial planning firm and some tech business but there was still one space left.

I mentally crossed my fingers and turned my face to his. "Oh yeah, what's it going to be?"

He smiled that smile and I got the dimple. "A doughnut shop."

"Oh my God! I love you!"

~THE END ~

*Continue the series now with **The Spark**!*
Or stay tuned for the first chapter to see what kind of trouble Fiona and Mark can cook up!

Stay up to date on Sylvie's upcoming books and projects by subscribing to her newsletter! http://bit.ly/NewsSylvie

Use these links to grab special **bonus** content!
http://bit.ly/BonusTheFix & http://bit.ly/TheFixCrossword

ABOUT THE AUTHOR

USA Today bestselling author Sylvie Stewart is addicted to Romantic Comedy and Contemporary Romance, and she's not looking for a cure. She hails from the great state of North Carolina, so it's no surprise that most of her books are set in the Tar Heel state. She's a wife to a hilarious dude and mommy to ten-year-old twin boys who tend to take after their father in every way. Sylvie often wonders if they're actually hers, but then she remembers being a human incubator for a gazillion months. Ah, good times.

Sylvie began publishing when her kids started elementary school, and she loves sharing her stories with readers and hopefully making them laugh and swoon a bit along the way. If she's not in her comfy green writing chair, she's probably camping or kayaking with her family or having a glass of wine while binge-watching Hulu. Or she's been kidnapped—so what are you doing just sitting there?!!

**Winner of the 2017 National Indie Excellence Award for Romantic Comedy

**Winner of the 2017 Readers' Favorite Silver Medal for Romantic Comedy

Thank you so much for reading *The Fix* – I hope you enjoyed it. If you did, a **review** on your favorite book site is always appreciated!

Want to stay updated on new releases, promotions and giveaways?
Subscribe to my newsletter! http://bit.ly/NewsSylvie

Want to hang out with me and my other readers?
Join my reader group on Facebook: **Sylvie's Spot - for the Sexy, Sassy, and Smartassy!** www.facebook.com/groups/SylviesSpot

Thanks! XOXO,
Sylvie

Keep up to date and keep in touch!
www.sylviestewartauthor.com
sylvie@sylviestewartauthor.com

facebook.com/SylvieStewartAuthor
twitter.com/sylvie_stewart_
instagram.com/sylvie.stewart.romance

EXCERPT FROM THE SPARK

Chapter One: Lucky

FIONA

"You must be so proud," yet another couple gushed while their eyes tracked me. Not that they were speaking to me, but everyone's eyes were always directed my way at these events. I was a bug under a microscope—a well-dressed and polished bug, but a bug nonetheless. I stood dutifully by as my parents received the compliment and my mother doled out air kisses to the couple decked out in expensive but understated formalwear.

Ugh.

We wouldn't want to go crazy and wear peek-a-boo lace or down-to-there necklines or, well, a color that actually stood a chance at catching someone's eye, now would we?

How inappropriate.

I didn't know how I was going to make it through another one of these yawn fests without at least something sparkly to look at. Come on, people! It was as if the invitations had read "Attire: Funereal Chic." My gaze swept the room—black, black, black—ooh, charcoal! Wait, *red*! Oh, just the exit sign—my bad.

I was stuck in this receiving line of sorts with nary a glass of champagne to keep me entertained. My only small act of rebellion was wearing the sexiest, skimpiest pair of lilac lace panties I could find, but they were completely hidden under my (modest, of course) black sheath Dior gown. I had forgone the delicious red patent leather Manolos—the poor things were stuck at home in my closet, probably happy they didn't have to endure this evening's event.

"Shut up, Fiona! Positive thoughts, please," my inner voice, Guilt, reprimanded.

Oh, right. *Sorry.*

So right now, you might be curious as to why I was the reluctant center of attention at this function, and you may even sympathize with me for having to stand here sans champagne and bored out of my mind (sexy panties aside). But in a minute, you're going to agree with Guilt and think I'm a bitch.

You see, when all these people approach my parents and say, "You must be so proud," what some of them really mean is, "You're so goddamn lucky and a tiny part of me resents the shit out of you." But it would be unseemly to actually say that so they always go with the former comment.

Regardless of etiquette, behind their eyes I can always see the envy along with the effort it takes to not let it show. They would give anything, and I mean *anything*, to have a daughter like me.

I know, what a bitch, right?

But it's the God's honest truth. Many of these couples would trade their very lives to have what my parents have—a daughter who survived childhood cancer and lived to tell about it.

"I thought that went exceptionally well, didn't you?" my mother asked as she perched on the sofa next to me, her makeup still flawless and her blond up-do as elegant as it had been five hours earlier.

"Definitely," I agreed, removing my shoes to massage my sore feet. I mean, I may not have gotten to wear the Manolos but I wasn't a heathen or anything—I had still worn a pair of stilettos. At five-feet and a quarter (you bet your ass I'm including that extra quarter inch), I always wear heels—the higher the better.

Fact: adults don't take short people seriously. So I do anything I can to even the playing field. If I had a nickel for every time I'd been patted on the head by some patronizing asshole, I'd be—well, I'm already rich, so let's just say I'd be *disgustingly* rich.

To be fair, I, myself, am not actually rich, but my parents are. And they both evidently got straight As in preschool because they are awesome at sharing.

We have this odd relationship where I just exist and they are so tickled that they throw money at me. That, in and of itself, would be pretty pathetic, but along with the money, they also throw unwavering love, affection, and support in my direction and I hope I do a halfway decent job of returning the same to them. Lots of people say they have the best parents in the whole world, but I actually do. And that, in short, is why I can never say no when they ask for my help with The Foundation. That and my ever-present companion Guilt, of course.

"Ah, there are my beautiful girls!" my father said as he entered my parents' massive living room. He'd loosened his bow-tie and removed his tux jacket and was now looking between us and the screen of his smartphone. "Guess how much we netted? Just take a guess!" From his excitement, the answer was clearly a good one.

"$350,000?" my mother guessed.

"Um, $375,000 and Barbara Rogers' hotel keycard—I hear 80 is the new 40," I said, earning a nudge from my mother.

My dad looked at me with the most serious expression he could muster. "Fiona, you know I won't go older than 75—at that point they're more housecat than cougar."

I giggled—what can I say? I'm a daddy's girl. Did I mention how awesome my dad is?

"So, drum-roll please," he said and my mother and I dutifully tapped our respective sofa arms. "$432,350!"

Mom and I enthused appropriately and my dad went to the kitchen to fetch a bottle of champagne—finally, I was going to get some bubbly!

"Totally exhausting, but so worth it," my mother sighed as she let herself relax back into the cushions of the stylish gray sofa, her formal gown somehow remaining completely un-rumpled. I propped my stockinged feet on the designer coffee table and pretended not to see the chastising glance aimed at me. "This is going to make such a difference—I think this may put us over the top to get the new MRI for Children's."

We speak in shorthand around here where medical terminology, facilities, and organizations are so ingrained in our everyday dialogue that I often wonder if we need complete words at all. We're like a depressing version of a teenage text exchange.

Everything is "WBC," "ALL," "SCT," "Children's," and "County" to name just a few. And it's a good thing because if we used all the actual terms, we wouldn't ever have time to finish a conversation. For instance, saying "ALL" is a lot easier than saying "acute lymphocytic leukemia," which just happens to be the disease that has defined and redefined our lives over and over.

All right, so here's the 4-1-1: When I was nine years old I was diagnosed with ALL, and because of a series of unlucky test results and poor response to treatment, it was revealed that my chances were quite shitty. Undaunted, my parents used every resource available to them and refused to let the poor prognosis stick. It took three hospitals, a clinical trial, every alternative form of treatment my mother could find on the internet, and finally a stem-cell transplant to put me in remission. When I tell you that acupuncture was the highlight of my treatment plan, you understand how much the rest of it sucked donkey balls. And anybody who tells you acupuncture is "fabulous" or "so rejuvenating" is a big, fat, lying whore. Just so you know.

Where was I? Oh, right.

Needless to say, we were all elated when we got the good news that my leukemia was in remission and we would finally be able to return to normal life. The only problem? There was no "normal" to go back to.

Suddenly, our whole family was grappling with a host of conflicting emotions. For the two years we'd been fighting the disease, we'd assumed the finish line was remission. Instead, we were almost paralyzed by the simultaneous onslaught of not just the joy, but also fear, guilt, and sadness. What if it comes back? Why did we reach remission when so many others didn't? What comes next? And what happened to the sense of innocence an eleven-year-old is entitled to?

It was at this point in my life that Guilt moved into my

consciousness and made herself comfortable. As far as I can tell, she spends her days tsk-ing disapprovingly at the cobwebs in my head and honing her skills as the most spectacularly annoying backseat driver ever. I would not recommend her as a house guest.

After a few weeks, I attempted to return to the life of a typical eleven-year-old, but everything was so different and awkward. My brain didn't seem to want to work the same anymore, and things that had previously come easily to me were suddenly overwhelming. I was having trouble remembering things, and my academic performance, which had always been stellar, began a downward spiral, with tests and homework becoming a huge struggle.

There were also physical implications from the disease and its treatment, the most noticeable of which was my development, or more specifically my lack thereof. While other girls my age were shooting up like beanstalks and wearing training bras, I was still essentially living in the body of a nine-year-old, with stunted growth and hormonal issues, neither of which would ever fully resolve—much to my dismay (see previous short-person rant).

In addition to all these issues, and possibly even because of them, my social life was a mess. My friends, classmates, and teachers treated me either like glass or like I didn't exist, their discomfort achingly obvious—which was all particularly hurtful to a young girl who had spent her childhood as a total people-person, embracing the world with complete exuberance and in the girliest manner possible.

I longed to return to the ease of my pre-cancer life but knew that I should just be happy to be alive. To ease the situation for everyone, I resolved to plaster a smile on my face so no one would think me ungrateful or worry about me. It was a habit I still maintained much of the time.

Meanwhile, out of a combined sense of gratefulness and contrition, my parents dove headlong into establishing a foundation for cancer research and childhood cancer facilities. To this day, it sometimes seems my mother's entire reason for existence is to spare other families the devastation wreaked by cancer. Other times, I'm reminded that about forty percent of her existence is actually reserved for worrying about me and trying to smother me —with love and attention. Although it often feels like plain old-fashioned smothering—you know, like with a pillow.

Obviously, my father is also very involved in what we call "The Foundation." But somebody has to bring in the big bucks, so he also runs the family's tech firm in Raleigh while my mom holds the reigns of The Foundation and I pitch in when called upon.

Then about four years ago, when I had reached my nine-year anniversary of remission, I decided to leave the nest—you know, the one full of pillows—and move to Greensboro to branch out on my own. I was twenty and finding it very difficult to find direction, so I figured becoming more independent might help me out.

My parents naturally fought it at first, but they eventually relented and bought me a gorgeous condo in a downtown high-rise with amazing floor-to-ceiling windows and two balconies. I freaking love it! They wanted to buy me a house, but I am way too much of a girly-girl to be responsible for my own appliances and grass and stuff. No thanks. I did mention the heels, right? Well, there is a whole designer wardrobe to go along with those heels and not a single pair of overalls in it. They also wanted to buy me a

Mercedes, but I talked them down to a Prius with a mere mention of environmental effects and carcinogens.

So, I had my own place and my own life in Greensboro, and it was only an hour and a half to Raleigh so my parents could still hover enough to keep them relatively content. The one thing I still didn't have, though, was direction. It apparently didn't come with the new life and new condo like a gift-with-purchase at Nordstrom. I've spent the last four years floating from job to job trying to figure out what I want to do with my life and having very little luck.

The floating around has, however, provided a couple of amazing benefits—some really hilarious and awesome experiences, and some really hilarious and awesome friends. The greatest of these is, of course, my best friend in the whole wide world, Laney.

She and I met when I was doing a brief stint as a receptionist at the same company she was temping for. At the time, Laney had been raising a baby, going to college, and working a part-time job.

Needless to say, Laney rocks, and I am in complete awe of her most of the time. She is a single mom to a five-year-old little heart-breaker named Rocco (Oh, excuse me, he now demands that I say he is five-and-three-quarters) and she almost ties my mom for being the best mom in the world. However, Laney's inability to wear stilettos or any article of clothing made from a material other than cotton will eventually result in Rocco growing up to marry a girl with similarly bad taste—and that's just irresponsible. Therefore, she rates second in the best mom competition.

What my best friend lacks in fashion sense, though, she makes up for in her taste in men. She recently scored herself one seriously hot man in the form of an adorably doting construction god named Nate. I often want to cry tears of joy at his love and dedication to Laney and Rocco—well that and his tight ass.

What? Laney doesn't care that I ogle him. Sometimes we even do it together. It's a bonding thing.

Laney has not had the easiest time since she accidentally got knocked up her freshman year of college and the douchebag dad essentially skipped the scene. So seeing her and Rocco with such a great guy does things to my heart. It almost makes me wonder if that's something I could want for myself. Almost.

But I have my condo and my various jobs and my flitting back and forth to Raleigh, not to mention Guilt to keep me company, so I'm good.

My phone vibrated on the coffee table next to my empty crystal flute, sending me reminders I'd need for the morning. This particular night of flitting to Raleigh was thankfully over and had ended just as I preferred—with a drink and the people I love. Celebratory champagne consumed and the night's events adequately dissected, my parents and I doled out goodnight kisses and decided it was time for bed.

The thought of driving back to Greensboro so late was unappealing at best, and with the bubbly coursing through me, would have been idiotic. I am not the most responsible person on a good day—Guilt can attest—and I have a healthy respect for my own limits, so driving would just be begging for trouble. Instead, I crashed in my old bedroom. This happens often enough that I keep a small wardrobe and stash of beauty supplies at my parents' house for just such times. I consulted my phone on the next day's plans and slipped into my nightgown. As soon as my head hit the pillow, I was out.

Thank God for champagne.

Oh right, and for letting me be alive.

Can I go to sleep now, Guilt?

The Spark by Sylvie Stewart is available in e-book and paperback.
Order your copy of ***The Spark*** today!

EXCERPT FROM THE LUCKY ONE

Chapter One: Hello, My Name Is Satan

BAILEY

"I swear his eyes are following me."

"It *is* a little creepy, I'm not gonna lie," said Mark, glancing over my shoulder.

A shiver ran down my spine and the hairs on the back of my neck stood at attention.

Mark took in my expression—which I'm sure was one of intense revulsion—and laughed right in my face, his straight white teeth not even attempting to bite his tongue. This was entirely unsurprising.

Mark's day is not complete unless he has tortured me in some way. He's the twin brother I never had and certainly never wanted. I already have an older brother, but Mark somehow worked his way into my life and I can't seem to get rid of him and his ridiculously bulky bod no matter how hard I try.

Still smiling at my pain, Mark shook his head and asked, "If he freaks you out so much, why the hell did you say yes?"

I glared at him, hands on my hips. "What in the hell was I supposed to do?! There were tears! Wet, sloppy tears!"

This did nothing to tame his smile. "You are such a fucking pushover," he whispered in my ear before skirting around me and approaching the creepy son-of-a-bitch.

"Ha!" I declared as I turned around, completely forgetting to keep my gaze averted. "Shows how much you know. I talked the kid down from a puppy!" I was actually quite proud of myself, despite my lack of forethought.

Turns out I can't stand lizards. Who knew? But the joyous expression on my nephew's face and the complete cessation of all waterworks was my prize to revel in.

Totally worth it.

I'm sure I broke every babysitting rule in the book, but desperate times call for desperate measures. It looked like my brother and his new wife just got themselves a pet gecko.

Whoops.

"Okay, little man. Everything is all set up," Mark said to a nearly-vibrating Rocco. "The light will keep him nice and warm, he's got a good place to hide in that log, and your Aunt Bailey will show you how to feed him the crickets." Mark's smile turned evil as his eyes found me again.

What in God's name had I been thinking? To be fair, I had assumed these crickets would be dead when the twelve-year-old sales associate had pushed his glasses up on his nose and mentioned we'd need to stock up. By the time I realized we would instead be bringing home a plastic container teeming with live insects, it was too late. Rocco, my adorable nephew, had fallen in love.

"Fist bump," Mark requested of Rocco, whose attention was completely captured by his new pet. Rocco extended his little fist without letting his eyes stray from the tank. "Thanks, Mark."

"Sure thing," Mark replied, ruffling the kid's dark hair. Then to me, "I gotta get back to Fiona."

"Is she feeling any better?" I asked, leaning against Rocco's dresser.

"Eh, hard to say."

Mark looked slightly distressed at the thought, and I marveled for the umpteenth time at the transformation my once-slutty friend had undergone since meeting his girlfriend, Fiona. Gone was the arrogant manwhore and in his place was an arrogant, pussy-whipped little douchebag. Ah, it warms the heart.

"I picked up an antibiotic for her, so hopefully that will start working soon," he said as he gathered his things.

I felt a sympathy pain in my throat just thinking about Fiona and her bout of strep throat. I cursed the damn virus for forcing me to step in and babysit Rocco while my brother, Nate, and his new wife, Laney, were off on their honeymoon. The same virus that, today, revealed just how ill-equipped I was to care for a child without becoming the biggest sucker known to man. "Well, tell her I hope she feels better and not to worry about Rocco—I got this."

Mark stopped in his tracks on his way to the door. He cocked his head, his eyebrows arching and his mouth sporting that damn smirk I wanted to knock off his stupid face. "Oh, I can see that."

I flipped him off, confident that Rocco's attention was elsewhere.

Mark's smug cackle echoed in the hallway outside Rocco's bedroom. "I'll let myself out!"

"You do that, Buffy!" Asshole.

Damn. It was just me and the kid again.

It's not that I don't like kids—I love my new nephew. I'm just not all that comfortable around tiny humans. I think I'm always waiting for them to judge me and find me inadequate somehow.

I'm the youngest of two kids, and I was never the babysitting type. My teen years had been spent sketching, reading, and plotting to get Nate in trouble whenever possible. And I'm a total daddy's girl, so I never pursued anything Riordan Murphy would consider "girly," much to my mom's disappointment. Babysitting, makeup lessons, and trips to the mall were eschewed in favor of hanging out at building sites with my dad and rocking out to heavy metal while painting and drawing. And, although my taste in music evolved as I reached adulthood, the rest pretty much stayed the same.

Everything I knew about taking care of a child consisted of lessons learned through trial and error over the last twenty-four hours.

I had been minding my own damn business last night, scarfing down cold pizza and channel surfing, when my phone had rung. I'd been ready to let it go to voicemail when I saw it was my brother. I hit the accept button; I should have let it go to voicemail.

The Lucky One is available in e-book and paperback.
Order your copy of ***The Lucky One*** today!

ALSO BY SYLVIE STEWART

THE SPARK:

Mark Beckett is the most annoying, patronizing, arrogant jerk on the face of the earth. So, naturally, I can't get the damn man out of my head.

FIONA:

Like the old saying goes, I'm a jill of all trades but a master of none. What I lack in skill, however, I make up for in enthusiasm—something certain people (ahem) find irritating. But I have my reasons for living my life the way I do, for diving into one project after another and trying to make a difference. And if Mark Beckett doesn't like it, he knows where to find the door. I don't need his approval … or his panty-melting kisses.

MARK:

I enjoy the simple things in life: a job well done, a cold beer, a hot woman … you get the idea. But there's nothing simple about the mess I just found myself in. The last thing I need is a pint-sized princess sticking her nose in my business and pushing every damn one of my buttons like it's her job. But Fiona Pierce may be the only one with the tools to solve my problems—and the power to change everything.

Order your copy of ***The Spark*** today!

THE LUCKY ONE:

Luck is no lady… in fact, she can be a downright bitch.

BAILEY:

Let's get one thing straight. I am not your typical girl. Sure, I've got all the parts, but I've been a stubborn, irreverent tomboy since the womb. Despite my Irish blood, bad luck makes a sport of messing with me, especially when it comes to men. But my shields are firmly in place now; nothing can touch me again. Except maybe Jake Beckett. He just might make this tomboy do the girliest thing in the world—fall head over heels in love.

JAKE:

I'm a pretty lucky guy. I have a phenomenal family, a career I love, and I'm building a brand-new life back in my hometown. And, not to be a jerk about it, but I do more than all right with the ladies. Everything's going according to plan—like I said, I'm a lucky guy. That is, until my luck runs out. Until I meet the girl I call "Irish." Irony can go kiss my ass.

Order your copy of *The Lucky One* today!

THE GAME:

They say opposites attract. Someone needs to tell that to Emerson Scott.

GAVIN:

All I ever wanted was to play ball. When an act of sheer stupidity took that dream away, I thought I'd never bounce back. But now I have the opportunity to coach an up-and-coming phenom, and I'm giving it all I've got. The fact that I've been lusting after his smoking-hot sister only sweetens the deal. Emerson may be buttoned up like a school librarian, but I play my best when I'm under pressure … and I *always* bring the heat.

EMERSON:

Never lose focus. Never lose control. Those are the first two rules in my carefully calculated plan for success. Finding myself thrown into the role of guardian for my little brother was *not* part of that plan. But I can adjust for Jay's sake; I'm not about to let one change make me lose sight of my goals. Too bad Jay's hot young baseball coach doesn't seem to give a fig about my plans. He has one of his own—and it includes me. Gavin Monroe may play like a pro, but that boy will never win this game.

Order your copy of *The Game* today!

THEN AGAIN:

It's been two years since the divorce papers slapped Jenna in the face, and it's high time to dive back in.

Step one: find a romance-novel-worthy man for a hot summer fling.

How hard could it be?

But disastrously bad flirting, a failed honky-tonk hookup, and a mix-up with one of Sunview's finest have Jenna seriously doubting if this is all worth it. Maybe she's better off leaving the world of love and sex to others—or maybe she's just looking in the wrong place …

Order your copy of *Then Again* today!

Made in the USA
San Bernardino, CA
24 December 2019

62342657R00144